Wishful Thinking

K. Crumley

Dragondreamz Publications

Wishful Thinking

K. Crumley

Printed Jan 2010

ISBN: 978-0-692-00725-9

For my loving Mimi,
my sister Tracy,
my niece Mia,
Aunt Kathy and Meghan.

And, in memory of my beloved grandmothers
Audrey Jane Patla
and
Laura Marie Crumley.

Death and Betrayal

Maevis stumbled, and then grasped the barre with pale trembling hands. She felt feverish and weak as she was warming up in the studio for the evening performance. She fought back the feelings of grogginess, willed away the haziness that filled her eyelids. *The show must go on.* Right at that moment, the artistic director entered the room. "Perfect timing," She said with a smirk. She already knew what he was about to say. Miguel was starting to sound like a parrot, repeating the same old lines.

"Easy old girl," he said. "Don't you think that's a sign that you should retire?"

"Not yet." Maevis replied, "I'll know when that day comes. But, believe me, it's a ways off yet."

"Every dancer's career has its expiration date." He said, "Even yours Miss Margot Fonteyn-of-Youth."

Maevis snickered at his weak attempt at humor. "Miguel, If I fall on my buttocks in the middle of the stage tonight then I'll—"

"You'll what dear?" He said, in a condescending tone. "Finally, step aside and allow one of the new upcoming ballerinas to have the spotlight?"

"You have ulterior motives," She said as she gained a bit of strength. "Look Tara, Bridgette or whatever young girl you're romancing this week will have her time in the spotlight soon enough."

Miguel's mouth dropped open, eyes grew wide. He put his hands on his hips. "Ahem!"

"Besides, this is opening night!" She protested, "You can't have some *understudy* just step into the principal role tonight! I've been rehearsing the role of *Giselle* for months now. I've worked hard for this!"

"Maybe a little too hard..." He countered, "You are what now? Thirty-five?"

"Thirty-two!" She said, hiding the fact that she felt injured and insulted. "Look, Miguel. I've put my heart and soul into this role. I'm not going to give it up to your little…starlet." With that, she stormed off into the dressing room and slammed the door. She was not ready to give up yet, even though it was wearing on her health. In that respect, she was truly her father's daughter.

That night the clouds rendered the stars invisible as Maevis drove home alone. Heavy rain beat down on her windshield. Her muscles ached from fatigue. The details of her conversation with Miguel still rang in her mind. But that was not the only thing that made her feel agitated.

Reese said that he had a late appointment that evening; and that he was unable to meet her at the Theatre to drive her home. She recalled the days when he would meet her back stage with roses and chocolates. Now, she felt a strange distance growing between them. It made her feel as if her heart was shattering within her chest—so many hopes and dreams were falling apart around her. Maybe deep down she should have known; a marriage like theirs would never last. They had warned her. She closed her eyes as hot, warm tears streamed down her face. "I wish that the heartache would end," Maevis whispered. "I wish that the trouble in our marriage would end."

She clutched the steering wheel with pale, sweaty hands. The downpour and the dark of night made it difficult to see the road ahead. As Maevis wished that she could see better through the heavy rain her windshield wipers beat faster and cleared away the water. Ominous light shone the way, as if it came from Heaven itself. In order to calm herself further she began to hum the music from *Giselle*. She'd heard it so many times these past few months with all the extra time she's been spending in rehearsal. She never grew tired of the bittersweet melodies.

The dizziness and nausea that she had felt earlier overcame her again. She was falling victim to the same disease her parents died from. These bouts of dizziness were more frequent, and lasted longer. Her skin more pale than usual, dark circles hung beneath her green eyes. Red hair, now damp from the rain, framed a thin, snowy white face. She weighed a mere 90 pounds. These bouts of malaise were only eased by sips of tea made from the petals of a rare floral plant. She couldn't wait to get home and have a cup.

At last, Maevis made the left turn onto 12th street, and headed towards her home. Something inside urged her to drive three more blocks to her family's Estate where her sisters lived. But, she didn't follow her intuition. Instead, she turned left onto a quiet street; towards the slightly more modest split-level home that she shared with Reese.

Her eyelids felt heavy as she let out a small yawn. Vision blurred as vertigo set in. The dampness of her hair and raincoat gave her an uneasy chill. The car pulled into the integral garage. She pushed the door open, and stood on trembling legs like a newborn colt attempting to stand. The car door swung shut. Coughing and gasping, she stumbled in the door. Damp, red tresses flung around her small elf-like face.

Maevis fumbled with her purse and satchel, and then wiped her feet on the mat. She pressed the button that closed the automatic garage door behind her. Maevis didn't turn the light on in the small hallway that led from the garage into the foyer. If she had, she would have seen an extra coat hanging from the coat tree next to her husbands. Unknowingly, she hung her raincoat right next to it; then slipped out of her wet shoes. Her satchel dropped to the floor. Her heart raced. Head was spinning. She felt a familiar itching, burning sensation on her back. Something was making her feel uneasy and nervous. She walked into the dark foyer. Stocking feet slipped on the ceramic tile as she staggered around in the darkness. Her trembling, white hand felt around on the wall for the light switch. She managed to find it and turn it on. She gasped, looking around. She sensed that someone else was in the house. "Reese," she called out "Reese?!"

Nobody answered. The house seemed strangely quiet except for a slight rustling noise that seemed to be coming from the upper level. She panicked, fearing that a burglar had broken in. In her weakness and malaise she wasn't strong enough to fight off an intruder. "Reese!" she called out, "Is...Is anyone there..." No one answered. She heard another rustling sound. Maevis came into the kitchen. Looking around she saw two wine glasses sitting on the counter. Each glass about half empty. One of them had a trace of red lipstick around the rim. "Reese...?" She called out again, her voice trembling. Her heart beat faster, as she feared another sort of intruder now—someone who would intrude on their marriage. A marriage once forbidden by her people, now held sacred by Maevis alone. She had to be brave. Whatever the circumstance, she had to handle it with courage. The room spun around her as she felt short of breath. A cold stream of sweat dripped over her pale forehead. The sound of a feminine giggle carried down the steps towards her as she headed toward the upper level. Maevis felt her face get warm, as rage the likes no human could see or feel swelled up within her. A strange new strength grew inside of her. It was a fury too strong for her to control. Wings fluttered and furled from her back, then spread out to their full span. The colors glowed brightly, iridescent rose and violet. Like a dragonfly's wings they fluttered and twitched, levitating her two feet off the ground. She flew into the room, to find Reese and his female client—a starlet named Bambi—in bed. The Faerie shrieked; the sound was inhuman. Eyes glowed like green lightening. She flew directly over their bed as a whirlwind from her wings blew all around.

"M...Maevis!" her husband said, trying to shield their naked bodies from the hurt, and furious Fae.

"She has wings!" The girl in the bed cried out, "*Wings* for God's sake!"

Maevis muttered something that they couldn't understand, something in her own native tongue. She felt as if she had lost control of both her power and her mind. The man she trusted with everything she had, and given up a great deal to be with had betrayed her. Suddenly, all of the objects of the room flew about in a ferocious whirlwind. The faerie shrieked again as green light shot out of her eyes. The girl in the bed screamed in fear. The husband tried to shield himself with a blanket. A book flew over his head, and hit into the bedpost. Picture frames flew off the walls. Perfume bottles shattered. Maevis remained levitated, spun uncontrollably, and drifted out into the hall. Debris showered down upon the victims of her wrath. Finally, Maevis fell to the floor, exhausted. Unconscious.

All three people in the house lay still for many hours, even as the rain subsided giving way to the morning sun.

🍂 🍂 🍂

A young woman bearing a striking resemblance to Maevis stood at the door, along with two teenage girls. One had reddish-blonde hair, pale skin and green eyes. The other was a tomboy, with short black wisps of hair framing an elfin face.

"Where is she?" The woman asked as she rang the bell of her sister's house.

"Maybe she's sleeping in, Fiona." The blonde girl replied. "I tried to call her last night, but there was no answer. She must have gotten home late or something."

"Ah, she's a sleepy head," The sable haired girl chuckled. "Maeve!" She called out as she banging on the front door.

"Shh. Cayden!" Fiona said, "You'll wake up the neighbors."

"Hey, it looks like *He* is home." The young blonde said, "I hope he at least had the decency to drive Maeve home last night. If not I'll—"

"Xandy, I don't care for the jerk anymore than you do," Fiona interrupted. "But try to be civil for Maeve's sake. God knows why, but she loves him."

Xandria just smirked. "Come on. Let's just go around to the side door." She said, as she trotted down the walkway that led to the side door, which lead into the hallway between the garage and the kitchen. Cayden and Fiona followed.

"Let this door be open," Xandria said. She tried at the knob, but it also was locked. She sighed, and put her hands on her hips. Then she smirked. "Open," she whispered. "Now."

The doorknob jangled; then the door swung open. Xandy grinned at her sisters. "Smart Alec!" Cayden said.

Xandria walked through the doorway that led into the hall, and then entered the foyer. Her sisters were right behind her. "Umm...did Maevis get a new coat?" Cayden asked as she noticed an unusual women's coat hanging on the rack.

"I don't think so," Fiona said. "Maevis would never wear animal fur."

She walked in quietly behind her two younger sisters.

"Maeve!" Cayden called out, "are you oh...oh my Gosh!" She ran through the hallway, up the steps to where her sister laid face down on the floor, wings now hanging limp; skin pale and ashen, "OH, Maeve!" Cayden cried, as she rolled her sister over to face her. "Wake up."

Fiona noticed the wine glasses on the counter as she passed through the kitchen, "Oh, no...not..." Then, strode up the steps, "Reese, you son of a—"

"Reese," Maeve whispered faintly, "He...and that girl..." Xandria rushed to her side, as she and Cayden helped her to sit up.

"Don't you worry about them, Maevis." Fiona said as her wings spread out, and began to twitch as she stormed into the bedroom, "I'll deal with that unworthy son of a—" Fiona stopped in her tracks, and screamed.

Xandria ran into the bedroom. "EW! Oh no, are they?!"

Two corpses lay in the bed side by side. Eyes open. Faces froze in an expression of shock and terror.

Cayden ran over to the side of the bed where her brother-in-law laid, and poked him to see if he would move. "Eew!" She gasped, "How gross! Did they like...die from...?"

"Eew." Xandria said. Then her eyes grew wide, "Oh...Maeve did you...?"

Fiona sighed, "Did you...Maevis, did you wish them...?"

Maevis sat still, looking pale and gaunt. As she looked up at her sisters, she stammered. "I don't...I don't know." Tears started to roll down her pale face, "I...I don't even remember...I cannot remember."

"No!" Cayden said, "You couldn't have. Not you!"

"You're not a killer Maeve." Xandria said, "Maybe they just received divine punishment? No less than they deserve really. *How dare* he cheat on you with that bimbo!"

"Girls," Fiona said. "This is serious. If the Council finds out about this we're all done for. Floraline, Rosalea, and the High Queen herself! They all told us we don't belong here—that we never should have come here. She warned our father that this would happen. It was a prophecy. Maeve and I both went against the council to marry wingless, non-magical men—now both men are dead. Both are dead *possibly* at the will of our spells!"

"I...I couldn't have," Maevis broke in. "I'll admit I lost control. But, I couldn't have said...." She started to sob uncontrollably.

Cayden ran back to her oldest sister, and helped her to her feet.

Fiona looked around the room, "I remember when Mom and Dad got really sick." She said, "Situations like this started to happen. They'd lose complete control. Things would fly everywhere! Cayden, when you were a baby you were almost hit by a flying lamp."

Cayden cringed.

Fiona continued, "Not on purpose, sweetie. They couldn't control their powers anymore. They got weaker and weaker. Sicker and sicker. Until they passed away. A faerie cannot live long in a world without magic. We're like fish out of water here."

"Yeah, fish out of water." Xandria said as she nodded. That expression had a special significance for her. She had, after all saved a mermaid from drowning last year. "Umm. In that case, I think we have to go home."

"NO!" Cayden said "I am not going!"

"Xandria is right, Cayden." Fiona said, "We might have to, at least for a while. Maeve is as sick as our parents were, and now Xandy has been getting sick too. We cannot live here forever."

"What about the Toy company, Fiona?" Cayden said, "I know Dad wanted to keep that going forever, that's why he left it to you. You're the reasonable one, the responsible one."

"Yeah," Xandria said. "You'll figure out something. You always do."

"Yes, I know. He was so..." Fiona smiled, thinking of her father. "So excited by this world. So enthused with what he could create. All the wonderful toys...He was genius. And it cost him nothing. He used magic to make them." She sighed. "Depleting more and more magical strength with each new creation..." Fiona stopped her pondering, sighed and then looked at the two bodies.

"Well, now." Fiona sighed, "First thing is first. We should call the police and just tell them we um...found them this way."

"NOT the police!" Xandria said, "As much as I hate to say this, we should see aunt Flo—"

"NO! Not her!" Cayden protested. "Not that witch! We should call the hospital and just say it's an emergency and that all four of us walked in and found them dead!"

"Cayden, we cannot lie." Maevis said, "The three of you weren't here. We'll just say that I found them in bed, and...and then I fainted—"

"And how would you explain all of this, Maevis?" Fiona said, indicating the state of the bedroom. "How would you explain this mess? How those two died?"

Xandria surveyed the scene, and the debris around the bedroom. "It might look like you hit them in the head with something."

Fiona continued, "Not only that, Maeve, If we call an ambulance and tell them you fainted they'll want to check you out as well. How would you explain the reason for your own fading health to some *wingless doctor*?"

"Um, just say she has the flu?" Cayden interrupted. "Some girl at school has it. It's going around."

"We could say I found them and went into shock," Maevis said as she moved into the kitchen.

She staggered but Xandria caught her and said, "Sit still. I'll make you a cup of tea."

Xandria helped Maevis to sit on a stool at the counter. She glared at those two half-empty glasses of wine. Then she turned her head. "Oh, I can't believe this! I can't believe he betrayed me!"

Xandria started the water for the tea and then brought down a jar from a shelf. Inside were pink flower petals, with a strong, sweet scent which filled the kitchen as soon as she opened the jar. The smell was very soothing. Maevis inhaled deeply, as some color returned to her face.

Each sister began to feel a surge of magical strength. Dragonfly-like wings furled from their backs resembling Maevis' yet each had its own unique hues. Cayden's shone gold and orange, which flattered her large, dark eyes and short wisps of black hair. Her elven face—usually bearing a spunky grin—still bore an expression of confusion and shock. Xandria's wings were iridescent blue and green, which seemed to match the color of her eyes. She crossed her arms and sneered in the direction of the bedroom, "creeps!" she muttered. "I'll never get married to a non-magical being! I swear it on my wings!"

The level-headed Fiona's wings of red and amber flared out and fluttered. "Don't worry Maevis." She said, "We'll straighten this out somehow. It's not your fault."

"Let her have some tea," Xandria said, "Wait until she feels a bit stronger. Then we can discuss this rationally."

The Investigators

The neighbors stared the way they always do in small towns; especially, when the neighbors are *just different*. These four sisters, were so gifted, beautiful, and had such a wide span in their ages. These girls almost seemed to have it all. And, they were considerably wealthy—their late father ran the largest toy company in the region. And, what intrigued them even more was that the oldest was regarded as a local celebrity.

"Did you know their father died only one day before their mother?" The lady with a brown bee-hive hairdo said as she stood outside the gate and watched the Etherwood sisters arrive home. "Look! They're bringing the oldest one with them. The ballerina. Wasn't she married too...?"

"Yes," a woman with a blonde bubble haircut and big plastic rimmed glasses answered, "I saw it on the news. He and some actress died in bed together! I wonder if she—"

"Oh, my gawd!" the bee hived woman answered, "Well she hardly seems capable of murder. I mean look at her. She looks like she hasn't eaten in years. Tsk. You know what they say about those dancers." She made a gesture with her finger, toward her mouth, emulating someone gagging themselves to bring up food.

"Ah, poor thing." The blonde said, as if she believed the implication of an eating disorder to be gospel truth.

Fiona glanced over at the gossips dismissively. She'd gotten used to them. However, today she resented their intrusiveness even more. She glared at them as she escorted her ill sister Maevis, wrapped in a shawl that covered her wings into the house. While she and her other two sisters could tuck their wings in,

Maevis was getting weaker by the minute and could barely control their flickering and twitching.

The girls headed up the walkway to the door of Etherwood manor. Before Fiona could get the key out of her jacket pocket, Xandria muttered "Open," and the door obeyed. Fiona shot her a glance, and then nodded in the direction of the nosy women. Xandy glared at them and then muttered, "I wish they would get a life."

Just then the bee-hived woman looked at her watch and said. "I just thought of something I need to do!"

"Yea," The bespectacled woman said. "Me too." Then, the two women walked back to their respective houses.

Maevis looked at Xandria and murmured a weak "Thank you."

Fiona nodded, and whispered "Thanks." After all, they had gone through enough scrutiny.

Earlier that day Fiona had dialed 911 and reported that there were two people found dead inside Maevis' home. The coroner had arrived shortly after, along with two plain-clothes police detectives and three uniformed officers. As these men began to rummage through the debris in the bedroom in search of evidence, the sisters walked outside to stay out of their way. However, as soon as the girls stepped out of the door they were bombarded by news media. Most of them would back off as Xandy would snap "No comment at this time," or "Look, my sister's not ready to talk." She put her arm around Maevis, and walked her to the car. They watched the coroners bring the bagged body of Reese Warren out of the house. Maevis shuddered, and shielded her face against Xandria's shoulder. As Fiona and Cayden got into the car, they watched them carry out the body of Bambi Templeton, wannabe theater actress.

"Guess she'll never make it to Broadway now," Xandria said.

"Oh, Xandy!" Maeve said, "That's so cold!"

That's so typical of Maevis, Fiona thought, as

she put the key in the ignition. *Even though the woman was stealing her husband she'd never think a cruel thought on her—let alone wish her dead.*

Fiona watched as the two detectives emerged from the house; then looked over at her car. She watched them whisper to each other and knew what they must be thinking. *They always suspect the spouse first,* she thought as she recalled when her own husband died in a drunken driving accident. Even in a case such as that, they suspected foul play because Roger was abusive and she was desperate to get away from him. She knew that they would be coming to the house later to question Maevis.

Fiona also had predicted that the media would swarm outside their estate like angry hornets. Maevis was an entertainer, and Reese was a high profile attorney representing many performing artists. Young Bambi was just getting recognition, and was starring in her first musical theater production. Fiona glared at the cameras, at the reporters pressing against the gate with microphones in hand. She could make them go away with a simple wish, but she just didn't have the strength.

However, Fiona realized that they had a lot more to fear than the police officers and the predatory news media. She worried about what Oberian Authorities would do when they found out about this. She and her sisters had undergone enough scrutiny when her own husband died. The human authorities had ruled it a drunken driving accident of course; but the Council still had their suspicions. They were warned sternly about the consequences of what would happen if another wingless man met his tragic death with the possibility of magical interference. Now there were two bodies loaded into the coroner's vehicle as it slowly rolled away—deaths that a faerie spell might possibly have caused. As she looked at Maevis sitting in the passenger seat, she worried for her. Maevis still claimed that she couldn't remember what happened or what she said. It was possible that Maevis could have inadvertently cast a wishful spell in the heat of her pain and anger; one that could kill her own husband. True Maevis was very in love with Reese. But, who knows how she felt last night when she saw those two in her own bed? Fiona sighed as she started the car; then drove her family home.

The car passed a row of large, yet modest two-story houses and then veered right onto 15th Street. It was clearly a more upscale neighborhood, with huge Tudor-style mansions and some more contemporary estates that were built recently. Their neighbors were mostly doctors and business men—and their busy body wives.

Etherwood Manor was probably the most exquisite estate in the neighborhood; a large, three story white brick mansion with lattice windows, which was fenced in on all sides. Brightly colored flora woven around the wrought-iron gate gave the Estate a certain other worldly mystique. It looked like something out of a fairy tale—quite fitting when you consider its inhabitants.

The Etherwood girls settled in, and tried to relax while drinking tea made from Yasminea. The inside was just as lovely as the exterior, with elaborate yet comfy furnishings. They sat on the cream colored leather sectional sofa, and relaxed. Cayden sat in the swivel armchair, of matching hue. The walls were pale cameo blue, enhanced with beige toned crown moldings. The fireplace was white brick, with a marble mantle decorated with artifacts from their home world Oberia and some family pictures. The peace was interrupted by the doorbell ringing. "I bet that's the police," Xandy said.

Maevis braced herself, knowing that she would be the one they wanted to talk to first—the wife. They always question the spouses first, believing they are the most likely suspects. Maevis had expected this, but she was still trembling. She bit her lip, and wondered, *how would I explain this to the police? How can I possibly*

explain what happened when I'm not even sure myself?
She recalled everything Fiona went through when
Roger died—but Fiona had always been the strong one.
Maevis sighed, and prayed for strength.

"Okay," She said, softly. "I guess I'm ready."

Fiona stood and walked to the door. As she
opened it, Maeve noticed the two detectives from
earlier were standing there. They flashed their badges,
and mumbled an introduction. Fiona invited them in
with a sweeping gesture of her hand. Fiona didn't seem
as nervous. If she was, it wasn't showing; unlike
Cayden, who sat playing with the string off her hoodie
and Xandria who sat with arms crossed, biting her lip.
Maevis knew that they had nothing to worry about—
she would be the one they focused on. With that in
mind, she stood up to greet them.

The taller, stocky man with light reddish hair
and a gruff expression spoke first. "I'm Detective
Barret Mulcahy." He reached out and shook Maeve's
hand. "This is detective Stan Browning." She nodded
in the younger, thinner man's direction. He had short
brown hair, and wire framed glasses.

Stan, smiled nervously. "Nice to meet you
Miss," He said as he shook her hand. He let go with
reluctance.

"So you were his wife." Mulcahy said.

"Yes," Maevis replied. "Loyal wife of eight and
a half years. Too bad the loyalty wasn't mutual." She
averted the detectives' eyes, as tears welled up in her
own. She tried to hide her pain from them. Deep
inside, Maevis wished that Reese was alive. She
wished that they had just one more chance to work
things out. But of all the spells that a faerie could
conjure up, she couldn't bring anyone back to life.
And, the thought that—in her anger—she may have
possibly caused his death was shattering her heart.

She glanced at her sisters. Xandy sat there with
arms crossed glaring with her know-it-all smirks at the
detectives. Cayden paced around, antsy. She hoped the
two younger faeries would behave themselves and not
wish something bad on the two detectives just to make

them go away, or play some silly prank. This was a very serious matter—the men were only doing their jobs, after all.

"Fiona could you get me some tea please?" She asked due to desperate need of Yasminea.

"Of course," Fiona said. "Can I get you gentlemen anything?"

"No thanks, Ma'am," They each said. Fiona departed into the kitchen as the questioning continued.

"Were you having troubles lately Mrs. Warren?" She was unfamiliar with people calling her by her husband's last name. She had retained her maiden name for career-oriented reasons.

"Oh, not any serious problems." Maevis replied, "We um…this past year we weren't spending a lot of time with each other." She shrugged, "I was afraid we were drifting apart. He didn't…just didn't have much time for me as of late. I just assumed it was his *precious career* that was getting in the way!" She began to sob. Xandria hugged her, consolingly. Browning, took a handkerchief out of his pocket, and handed it to Maevis.

"There now, Miss…" He said, "It's okay…That! That pig! How could he cheat on a lady like you?"

Mulcahy shot him a stern glare. He cleared his throat, reminding his partner to act professional. "Yeah, damn shame." Mulcahy continued, "Did you know her? The girl. The actress."

"I knew *of her*. That was it." Maevis said with a smirk, "She took a dance class at the Ballet Company about two or three years ago. She was clumsy and awkward. She claimed that tap and jazz were more 'her thing' But some how I cannot see her being that good at any style of dance." Maeve managed a wry grin "Lovely singing voice though. He was working on a recording contract for her—"

"Like a siren, she lured him away with the sound of her voice." Xandria said, "Or so I'd guess."

Mulcahy looked at Xandria, raising his eyebrows. "Oh, you knew of her too?"

Xandria tilted her head. "I heard of her." She clarified, "Why?"

"Just curious." He said, "Did you know of the affair?"

"No. I only knew my brother-in-law was a louse!" Xandy said, getting to her feet. Her hands on her hips. "I didn't *have to* know that he was having an affair to know that he's not good enough for my sister. He was never worthy of her."

"Xandy, please…" Maevis interceded.

Just then, Fiona came in with the cup of tea. Glancing at Xandria, she cleared her throat. Cayden seemed less bored. She sat there grinning, on the edge of her seat.

"What do you mean, not good enough?" Mulcahy asked, again.

"He was not worthy of a—"

"Xandria!" Fiona spoke up, glaring at her with the expression of a school librarian hushing a noisy student.

"He wasn't worthy of an Etherwood sister, let alone a Prima Ballerina." Xandria concluded, with a smart-alec grin.

Maevis sighed, relieved that Xandria didn't blurt out that they were Faeries. Their magical abilities would only make the detectives more suspicious.

"Fair enough assessment," Browning said, nodding. It was as if he was in agreement. Maevis felt him staring at her, and it made her uncomfortable. The older officer seemed to notice this too. He frowned at Browning, elbowing him. Xandria didn't seem to think too much of it. But, Maeve could tell by the look on her face that she wanted to continue her rant. Fiona seemed guarded, afraid that the detectives were going to pry too deeply and find out something that they shouldn't. Cayden remained the observer.

"Mrs. Warren," Mulcahy continued.

"Please, call me Maevis." She said.

"All right then, Maevis." He said, with a nod. "Please tell us what happened when you came home that evening."

Here we go, Maevis thought. Xandria sat down next to her and held her hand. Cayden began fidgeting with the zipper of her hoodie. Fiona sat in the armchair, hands folded on her lap. "I came home late that night, after ten. I had a performance. It was raining. I—" She started to sob again as she remembered what she wished for in the car. *I only wished for our problems to end…*She thought, *but not for his life to end.*

"That's okay," Browning said, "Go on. Take your time."

"It was storming." She said, "And I was tired. I was not feeling well. I hated driving home alone at night…" She said.

"Did it make you angry?" Mulcahy asked.

"No, it made me sad." She replied, "Very sad."

"What happened when you got home?" Mulcahy asked, as if he wanted to cut to the chase.

Maevis composed herself for a minute. She cleared her throat and then continued. "I walked in through the garage, and felt like something wasn't right. I knew somebody else was in the house. I was afraid it was a burglar. I called out Reese's name a couple of times. He didn't answer. But I heard a noise coming from the bedroom. Then I saw two glasses sitting on the counter. Wine glasses. I realized what was going on, so I went into the bedroom…" Maevis' voice trembled, "I saw them in bed together!"

"And then…?" Mulcahy pressured, despite the nudge from his partner.

"Then I screamed! I…." Maevis guarded her words. "I had some sort of tantrum. I think I scared the girl. She started screaming too. I left the room. Ran out into the hall, and I fainted."

"Fainted, huh?" Mulcahy said, sounding skeptical.

"Yes." Maevis said firmly, looking him in the eye. "I fainted right there in the hallway."

"When you came too…?" He asked.

"It was the next morning, when my sisters came in." She said, "I could barely remember what happened. I just kept seeing them in my mind. Seeing him *with her—"*

"And, can you girls collaborate this?" The detective said, glancing around at the other three ladies.

"Yes," Xandria spoke up first. "When we came in, Maevis was passed out on the floor in the hallway."

"She didn't know what happened." Fiona said, "It was just as big of a shock to her as it was to us, when we saw…*those two* lying there."

"Bastards," Cayden chimed in.

"Cayden, watch your language in front of these two gentlemen." Fiona scolded.

"Sorry, guys." Cayden said.

"That's excusable given the circumstances," Browning said, with an understanding smile.

Finally, Mulcahy cleared his throat. "Look, everybody is really emotional right now." He said, "I think we ought to let these ladies get some rest. Come on, Stan. We got work to do."

"Um…yeah." He turned around, and smiled at Maeve, shook her free hand. For a moment there she swore he was going to raise it to his lips and kiss it. "Nice meeting you, Maevis."

Maevis managed a slight smile, "Nice meeting you too, despite the circumstances detective."

Fiona saw the detectives to the door.

So as the two men left the Etherwood Manor, Xandria felt relieved. She sighed, and then let out the way she felt. "Well, glad that's over with." She said, "I think the skinny one was sweet on you Maevis. And I think he agrees with me. Reese and that wannabe-actress got what they deserved."

"Xandy, we know how you feel." Fiona continued, "But our sister loved him. Please try to be at least a little compassionate."

"I am!" Xandria spat out, "I am being compassionate for her. But I don't feel sorry for Reese and that girl. He was cheating on her with that second-rate musical theater bimbo!"

"But he didn't deserve to die right there on the spot." Fiona said.

"And, Maevis certainly didn't deserve to find them there," Cayden chimed in. "She doesn't deserve to be accused of a murder she didn't commit!"

"Of course she doesn't." Xandy said, "She doesn't deserve any of this. None of us do. I hate to say it. Grandmother was right. We never should have come here! I just wish we could go back! I wish none of this ever happened! I wish she had never married Reese! I wish Fiona had never married that drunken Roger! I...I wish...." She closed her eyes, stomped her foot. A vase holding lilies fell off the end table and landed on the ground, breaking. A mirror fell from the wall, shattered as it hit the ground.

Cayden screamed.

"Xandria, just calm down!" Fiona said, "Everything will be okay."

"No it won't," Xandria cried. "Why isn't it working? Why aren't my spells working? I've wished several times that we could just go home, where our people can thrive and live in peace...away from all of these wingless folk, and their money, and pettiness, and nosy ways, their judgmental eyes watching us...But...it hasn't happened." She sighed. "We're faeries for Heaven's sake! Aren't all of *our wishes* supposed to come true?"

"Sometimes, we are just too weak for any of our spells to work." Maevis sighed, "Like now. This is the weakest I've ever felt." She sat on the sectional, leaning back. She looked pale and fragile.

Xandria felt embarrassed for her outburst—but at least her feelings were made known. She never liked Reese—she never really cared for non-magical people. She just wanted to go home; and felt that at a time like this they really should.

"Look Xandria, I understand." Fiona said, "We should probably all go back to Oberia at a time like this. But we can't right now—"

"Why?" Xandria said, "Because of Ballet? Because of the toy company?"

"Because something is preventing us." Fiona said, "Some strange magical force has managed to hold us back and keep us from walking right through the gate."

"No," Xandria protested, "That can't be true!"

"I'm afraid it is, sweetie." She said, "Two days ago Maevis and I went to get some more Yasminea…but something was preventing me from just walking through the gate to Oberia."

"But, that cannot be!" Xandria said, shaking her head.

"I'm afraid so," Maevis said, "Somebody put a powerful spell on the gate—"

"But who would do such a thing?" Xandria said, "Who would be so cruel as to prevent us from being where we are healthy, happy, and above all safe?"

Cayden's eyes narrowed as she said "Who do you think?"

Aftermath

That evening Maevis retired to her old bedroom. She looked around at the satin dance shoes that still hung on the wall, along with posters advertising many of the Ballet Company performances. Porcelain dolls sat on the shelves, and a picture of her with her family at her first ballet sat on the dresser. She looked at it and smiled as she remembered her childhood. She'd had a very traumatic day and her mind was still flashing back to the night before. She couldn't get the vision of her husband's handsome blonde head, frozen in an expression of shock lying on the pillow…next to *her.*

Maevis tried to relax and put it out of her mind. She undid the clip from her long, auburn hair and started to comb it out. *I just cannot believe that he's gone,* she thought to herself. *Everything in my life is going to change now.* She was overwhelmed by vast uncertainty. Of one thing she was sure of; she'd move back into this house with her sisters. *Maybe Xandria is right. Maybe we should really go back to Oberia… But what about the ballet? My career means so much to me. And, how better to deal with Reese's death and infidelity than by pouring all of my time and energy into each performance—Giselle, of all ballets. The story of a young girl betrayed… Who became a Wylie of the woods…* She contemplated the irony.

Then, she considered what the negative publicity could do to her career. *I can endure the whispers at the rehearsals, and in the practice studios and dressing rooms. I'm used to that by now. Women can be so catty. Come to think of it, so can most of the men…*

She can only imagine what they would be buzzing about in the theater—growing silent the moment she came into the room. Wondering if she did what *they think* she might have done, some even hoping for the worse case scenario just to bump her out of the top spot. *I'm used to hearing "when's the ole' girl going to retire", but this is different...*

Suddenly, Maevis sensed someone's presence; broke her chain of thought. She jumped, then turned around to see who it was. "My Gosh," She exclaimed. "You frightened me half to death!"

"You ought to be frightened," said the stern-looking faerie standing behind her. Long, gray hair matched her pale, ash colored wings. She wore a long, blue gown trimmed in white ribbon with a crown of silvery petals on her head. "You do realize what you've done?!"

Maevis was flustered, "Aunt Floraline, I—"

"This is the second time now that a wingless man has died after marrying one of you!" The old faerie said, "Do you realize what this means?!"

"Floraline, I ...." Maevis stammered. Her face felt warm. "I don't know if I ....I was angry! I was frightened! He betrayed me, and—"

"Oh, of course he did, my dear. You married a weaker being, after all." Floraline laughed, despite her stern demeanor. "Those wingless. Tsk. They could never appreciate a faerie. And I had warned you and Fiona that nothing good could come from associating with them. Let alone *marrying them!*"

"But, you know that Roger's death was not Fiona's fault...nor..."

"Oh, so she claims!" Floraline grew even more pompous, crossing her arms and glaring at Maevis. "So you all claim. Just because the Outer Realm's authorities have declared the death accidental doesn't mean the Faerie Council has. You—any one of you—could have wished this on her husband. Or, your husband for that matter."

Maevis stood up and raised her voice, "Accidents happen with or without magical intervention."

"Yes, they do." Floraline said, "However, we must keep in mind that this is the second husband that has died in this family. And, given the circumstances of your husband's death? Well, the Council is up in arms over this! They'll want to see you about this matter very soon. All four of you."

"Of course," Maevis said. Her green eyes met her aunt's cold, grey eyes. "Just let us know what date and time. We'll be there." Maevis turned away from her and sat back down, feeling no need to show any customs of respect for this woman who has taken over the kingdom since their Grandmother's health began to fade. Maeve's father Penley should have rightfully been king. And, he would have if he had survived. Maevis was unaware if her grandmother had named a new heir.

They had lived in the Outer Realm so long, in fact since Maeve and Fiona were just little girls. Their Grandmother rarely left Oberia. The Queen was quite elusive, especially given the recent state of her health.

"I will let you know the day and hour after my next meeting with the Council." Floraline said, "Until then *fallen child*, farewell!" Then with a dramatic gesture of her arms and wings, she disappeared.

Maevis cringed, and muttered "Witch" under her breath as she threw her hairbrush at the spot where her sanctimonious aunt had stood just seconds before. Her pulse raced as she ran her hands through her long red hair. She felt agitated and angry, even though this was expected. She knew she would be facing suspicion and accusations from both local law enforcement and the Faerie Council.

As she sank back into the chair in front of her vanity, she felt discouragement and vulnerability overcome her. Maevis realized that the police could never prove her guilty as there was no forensic evidence—unless they claimed that she threw around all of the belongings in the room and managed to hit them over the head. But, it was the Faerie Council that she feared the most. After all, banishment could not only lead to her shame, but to her death. Floraline had called her a "fallen child." Someone who would kill of a defenseless, wingless human using magic; a sin deemed unforgivable. But Maevis would never do that;

at least not consciously. That was the problem that faced her now. Maevis couldn't even remember what she had done or said…what she had wished…what spell she might have inadvertently cast. The whole evening was a blur. She remembers being awoken by her sisters early in the morning, and discovering Reese and that actress were dead in her bed. *It couldn't have been my fault?* She wondered, *Could it? I'd never wish him dead. I loved him too much. Yes, he cheated on me. Ha. For all I know Bambi wasn't the only one…who knows how many…*the thoughts spun around in her head, making her angrier. Dizziness overcame her. She began to tremble. A porcelain figurine few off the dresser and smashed against the wall, making her jump. Maevis went over to the bed and lay down, trembling until consciousness slipped away.

🍂🍂🍂

Cayden kept to herself the next day at school. This was easy enough since she found it hard to fit in amongst the wingless—especially the girls. She heard Patty Delani and Shari Morris snicker as she walked past. Normally Cayden never let those cheerleaders bother her. She always was laughed at, being a tomboy with short black wispy hair and wearing jeans and sweatshirts. Cayden fit in better with the kids she played basketball with in the park. She was not your typical girlie teen, and proud of the fact. She was also proud of the fact that she carried her own personal brand of revenge against the prissy teen queens.

"Did you hear…her sister killed…the…" She heard them say in hushed voices.

"Terishah!" she whispered, as she walked past the catty brats. Then, Shari screamed as one of her fake fingernails had fallen off, causing her to bleed profusely. She ran down the hall in the direction of the nurse's office squealing. Cayden grinned, impishly. After all, the girl wasn't in any real harm. However, Cayden knew she would get into trouble with Maeve and Fiona if they found out about this. They warned her

to stop casting spells at school—especially now. They were under enough suspicion from the Council, and didn't want any more trouble.

Cayden headed into the classroom, and plopped down in her seat. She thought about what she done with little regret. *Not as if I killed her*, she thought. *And, the way she screamed was quite funny. Girlie-girls make such a big deal over stupid things like fake, plastic nails and "perfect" hair. Hmm, maybe I should turn her hair a pukey bluish-green next time.* Cayden meant no harm; she was just a prankster. She sat at her desk and eyed the other kids. Her back itched from her wings being tucked under her hooded sweatshirt. She'd love to see the reaction of her fellow students if she would let them unfurl. She'd love the shocked look on all their faces. However, she realized that it was not a good idea to reveal her true nature to her classmates.

The whispering in the classroom died down as Miss Rivera entered the room. She smiled and greeted the class. Miss Rivera was one of the few wingless folk that Cayden actually liked, which made attending this school five days a week a little more pleasant.

The teacher was just starting to talk about the next book they would be reading for class when someone knocked at the classroom door. As she went to answer it, Cayden leaned up in her chair to see who it was. Miss Rivera seemed taken aback to find two police detectives standing there, showing their badges. Cayden recognized the two men as Barret Mulcahy and Stan Browning, and realized they must be there to speak to her. She slumped down into her chair a little bit. The teacher stepped outside to speak to the two gentlemen. Then she came back in the room, and walked over to Cayden. "Yes, Miss Rivera?" she asked.

The young teacher leaned forward as if what she said was in strict secrecy, and not to be heard by the other classmates in earshot "There are two police detectives outside asking to speak to you." Cayden could tell by the tension in her voice that she had heard about her brother-in-law's death.

"All right." Cayden said, managing a smile despite her nervousness. She arose from her desk, and headed toward the door.

A few students let out a collective "uh-oh" as they always did whenever someone was in trouble. She was used to it. She was always in trouble for something or other. Just not like this. Not with the police.

She walked out into the hall to meet the two detectives. They were apparently investigating the deaths of Reese and that girl Bambi as if it was a double-murder. Cayden sighed as she prepared herself to answer their questions knowing that she had done nothing wrong. *I'm only a kid after all, what could they possibly want to ask me?* She wondered. *I wasn't even there.*

"Ms. Etherwood," Mulcahy asked her, "Is there somewhere we can talk that is a little more um…private?"

Cayden could tell that the students milling around in the halls made him nervous. "I think the study hall next to the library should be free." She said, "Follow me." She nodded in the direction of the hallway veering left, and then walked in that direction. The detectives followed her. She led them into a small room, right next to the library. It didn't have typical desks, but small couches, armchairs, and coffee tables. Aside from the clutter of textbooks, library materials, and cans of soda set scattered about that the room was relatively clean and neat. She sat down on an armchair, and gestured with her left hand for the officers to sit on the couch straight across from her. The heavier fellow sat down in the chair across from her. The younger, skinny detective fiddled with his glasses then took out a notebook and pen and sat down. The older man began asking the questions. "So Miss Etherwood…"

"Please, sir. Call me Cayden." She said.

He grinned, "Okay, Cayden. Tell us where you were last night around nine thirty pm."

Cayden could only guess that that was the time that they estimated that her brother-in-law and that actress died. "I was at home. Well, I played basketball with my friend Mitchell until eight O'clock. Then I went home. Fiona gets upset if I stay out any later than eight."

"Ooh, so you live with Fiona, not Maevis?" He inquired, "Even though Maevis is the oldest?"

"Yeah, well it was our parent's house," She said, "Maevis moved out when she got married."

"Wasn't Fiona married also?" He asked.

"Yeah, but her husband lived with us too." The subject of Roger made her uncomfortable. She shifted in her chair, and tugged at the string of her hooded sweatshirt. "That is, when he wasn't in jail, or something. He was an alcoholic. He beat her a lot." She hung her head, and averted the detectives' eyes.

"So we heard." Mulcahy said. The younger officer was taking notes. "But tell me about your other brother-in-law, Reese Warren. What did you think of him? Did you get along with him?"

"Well, I always tried to be nice to Reese." She said, looking up again. "I didn't hate him. He was nice to me at times, but really aloof and snobby. Like he thought he was better than everybody else."

"Did you know Bambi?"

"The deer?" Cayden said, flashing a cocky grin. "I saw that movie when I was a little kid."

"No, you know who I mean!" He smirked. The tone of his voice let her know that he had no patience for a smart alec. "His girlfriend. The actress."

"I had no idea who she was," Cayden said with a shrug. "And, now that I know—well I think she is a skank. But, she's dead now. Does it matter?"

"Well, sort of." The younger man spoke, "Did you know about their affair? Did you ever see her around?"

"No," Cayden said. She shifted in her chair again, twirling the string of her hoodie around her finger. "I thought he loved Maevis. Why would he take some actress wannabe over my sister? Maeve is a…" Cayden almost slipped, and said Faerie Princess. "She's a Prima Ballerina after all. Besides, Maevis is more beautiful."

"Yes she is." Browning said bearing a nervous grin. He fumbled with his note pad and pen. Cayden grinned, realizing that Browning had a crush her sister.

Mulcahy elbowed his partner, "Cayden, when did you discover the bodies?"

She cringed at the word bodies, then said, "Same time that everyone else did. When we showed up at Maevis' place the next morning."

"Did any of you try to revive them?"

"I um…I thought they were just sleeping." She said, "I tried to poke him and wake him up. He was stiff and cold. It was freaky."

The detectives looked at each other and nodded.

Cayden rambled, "I never saw a dead human before. It was really gross. I wish it didn't happen. I think that…I just think that something weird went on. Maybe they saw Maeve coming in the room and freaked out and had heart attacks. Or maybe they did it so much they had heart attacks? Gross."

The two investigators chuckled. "Okay, kid. That would be all the questions we have for you." Mulcahy got up and shook her hand, she smiled a little. "Thanks"

"You're welcome." The girl said.

Browning shook her hand too, "I hope Maevis is feeling better." He said, "She seemed pretty shaken up yesterday."

"Yes, she was." Cayden confirmed, "She hasn't been feeling well lately. She's not going to be performing tonight. She's been through too much and needs her rest."

"That's a good idea." Browning said.

"Okay, we're done here." Mulcahy said as he nudged his partner. "Have a nice day, Cayden."

"You too, sir." She said as she left the room, headed back to class.

🍂🍂🍂

"Well, that explains why the kid's finger prints were all over the place." Mulcahy said, as they exited the school and walked towards their car. "She tried to wake him up." He stifled a snicker.

"She said dead *human!"* Browning muttered, "What do you think she meant by that?"

"I don't know." Mulcahy said, "Maybe she was too young when her parents died to remember seeing their bodies."

"Could be," Browning said. "Maybe she's only seen dead animals before…But the way she said 'humans' was so weird, like she considers herself above human."

"Yeah, I picked up on that," Mulcahy said as he shook his head. "Heh. Kids, today."

"So, how's the wife feeling today?" Stan's voice softened.

"Oh, about the same Stan," Barry said. "She didn't take too well to the chemo. She was up sick all night." The stern, gruff man put his hand to his face as he started to cry.

Stan put his hand on his partner's shoulder, "It's okay, buddy. She's going to get through this. She'll be fine. I'm praying for her and so are my parents."

"Aw, thanks man. It's appreciated." He replied as he tried to compose himself. After a several minutes of silence he said, "well what's our next move?"

"I think we should talk to the second-youngest." Stan said, "The Strawberry blonde. She had the worse attitude and—"

Mulcahy sighed and glared at his partner. "You really don't want to believe the wife could be guilty, do you?"

"Maevis hardly seems the type, Barry." Stanley said, "She's too…Too gentle. Charming…"

"Look, Romeo, this isn't a dating service." Barry said, "This is a criminal investigation. Don't go crossing somebody off the suspect list just because you're taking a liking to her." He knew his partner very well. He had seen him go through this before. In Barry's opinion a few women who might have been guilty had gotten away with crimes and misdemeanors because of Stan letting his feelings get in the way during an investigation. "Still, I think you're right. That strawberry blonde had an attitude on her. She wasn't particularly fond of her Brother-in-law at all."

🍂🍂🍂

While Xandria was sitting on her bed reading a book, she began to feel dizzy. The book fell to the floor. The room seemed to spin around her. Her trembling hands reached for a small box on her night stand. Before she could reach it, she had passed out cold.

Her unconscious mind dreamt of Sirenia—of her captivity on that pirate's ship. The mermaid princess, dying in a tank drained of water. "Don't worry. I'll get you out of here!" Xandria said, "I'll get us both out." She heard the cruel pirate's footsteps stomping down the stairs. Her heart raced from fear and panic. Xandria had one last resort and she wasn't even sure it would work. She took the crystal pendant from around her own neck, and put it around the mermaid's neck. Then, Xandria grasped the crystal in her hand and whispered something in the language of the Fae...

The mermaid started to breathe easier, and appeared to be revived. "Hurry...he's coming!" She whispered hoarsely. His footsteps pounded on the steps. The mermaid held Xandria's hand, "Hurry!"

"Ishana!" Xandria's sense of panic increased. Her heart pounded in time with his footsteps. The sound of which was getting closer. The ship shuddered, and swayed. Something was wrong. Her spell wasn't working. "Ishana! Ishana!" She repeated with urgency. The mermaid clasped her hands around Xandria's and chanted a spell of her own. Then suddenly, a bright orb of light formed around the two young women as the ship rocked violently...

With a gasp, Xandria awoke. As she looked around, she felt relieved that she was still lying on her bed; though the echoes of the pirate's feet on the steps seemed to follow her into consciousness...until she realized where that sound was coming from.

Oh, the door?! She thought. She got up to answer it, and fell to the floor. Looking down at her legs, she saw that they were covered with pink scales. She now had flippers for feet. "Not now." She said, rolling her eyes. Like Maevis, Xandria was also losing control of her magic. She crawled over towards the night stand unable to walk with her flipper-feet. She reached for her teacup. The knocking at the door continued. A framed picture of the family flew across the room, and crashed up against her dresser. "It just figures!" she said, as she realized her cup was empty and threw it aside. She leaned on the nightstand as the room continued to spin. There was something other than Yasminea that could be her saving grace at a time like this. Her trembling fingers reached into her porcelain trinket box, and pulled out a long silver chain with a crystal orb dangling at the end of it. Inside the orb a tiny bit of Yasminea floated in water.

The pounding at the door continued. Whoever it was grew more persistent. "COMING!" she shouted, as she managed to reach up and hit the intercom. Xandria slipped the necklace on and instantly felt a resurgence of strength. She concentrated. The scales and flippers disappeared from her legs. She stood as she fully regained her strength. Then, as Xandria headed downstairs to answer the door, she noticed her wings were still unfurled. "Down." She said, as they were again pressed flat against her back hidden under her pink blouse. "On my way," she called out as she reached the bottom of the steps, "be patient, whoever you are!" She reached the door, and opened it. "Oh, hello detectives."

"Hello, Xandria." Detective Mulcahy said.

What do they want, Xandy wondered. *Hadn't they already asked enough questions the day before?*

"Is Maevis around?" The younger one asked. She saw the older man nudging his partner.

"No, she isn't here...she's um..."

"That's alright," The stocky older officer said. "We're here to speak to you anyways."

Xandria's eyes widened. A lump rose in her

throat. *Why me? What would I know that could help their investigation?*

"Oh? Well okay." She said, "Come on in then, and sit down. Would you like something to drink?"

"No, this won't take long." Detective Browning said, "We promise. We just want to ask you a few questions related to your brother-in-law and that theater performer."

Xandria sighed, "All right." She was nervous. *Do they suspect me?* She wondered. *They cannot suspect me. I wasn't even at Maeve's that night. And, I had no idea about Reese's affair, and even if I did— Even if I had wanted to kill him, I wouldn't have had the magical strength to successfully wish anybody dead.* Even so, Xandria knew that if she did, she would never be able to go back to Oberia. In fact, it was her desire to live there permanently. She just doesn't belong here. Every day it became more painfully obvious. In fact, in light of recent events—and with Maevis being as sick as she was—she was quite sure that none of them belonged in this non-magical realm.

The two detectives sat down on one side of the sectional sofa. Mulcahy began to speak. "When we talked with you ladies yesterday, you didn't seem too fond of your brother-in-law."

Xandria sat down on the arm chair across from them, and then replied "Well. No, I wasn't." She guarded her words. "Maevis was too good for him." *Yeah, I hated him. But that doesn't mean I killed him*, she thought to herself.

"Did you know about their affair," He said, "his affair with that theater actress?"

Xandria looked Mulcahy in the eye, and spoke bluntly. "No. I had no idea. I thought he was despicable—but I didn't know he was *that despicable.*" She leaned back, crossing her arms in front of her. "He was never there when my sister needed him. Ever. He used to just come around every premiere or opening night just to act like he was husband of the year. Like some big-shot."

"Oh, I see." The younger man said, "Sounds

like he wasn't much of a husband."

"No." She said. "He wasn't"

Mulcahy chimed in again. "Well, Xandria, Where were you the other night about nine o'clock pm?"

She knew this question was coming. "I was here at home. Upstairs reading. You can ask Fiona." She winced, "I didn't like being around Reese at all. I would have gone to Maeve's performance except I feared he'd be there." She shook her head, rolled her eyes. "Hm! I should have gone! I should have guessed he wouldn't be there. Not like he is there for her *anymore*, anyways. He was a jerk. But at least he's gone. Now, Maevis doesn't have to worry about him anymore. She doesn't have to feel bad that he's not around. And as for that bimbette he was with, well apparently she got what she deserved to." *Oops, I shouldn't have said that.*

Xandy got nervous, started fiddling with the appliqué on the arm of the chair, and wondered if the two detectives could tell how anxious she was.

The two officers looked at each other. "Xandria, were you home the entire night?"

"Yes, I was." She replied.

"And, during the day?" Mulcahy asked; he pressed for more details.

"I went out for a bit…into the woods…just for a walk. Then I came home. I read a book, took a bath, and then laid down a bit. I wasn't feeling well—"

"And, you didn't go over to Maevis' house at all?" He pressed.

"No, not that day—"

"And you weren't suspicious at all," Mulcahy persisted, "That your brother-in-law was having an affair."

Xandria answered calmly, and honestly, "I was suspicious that he was up to something. But I wasn't sure what it was. If I had known, then I would have told Maevis."

"Ah, okay Xandria." Mulcahy stood up, "We'll be in touch."

She got up and walked them to the door, "Alright, detectives." She said.

She felt uncomfortable and feared she made herself look guilty.

The detectives shook her hand as they turned to leave. "Tell Maevis I hope she's feeling better." Detective Browning said.

"Okay, I will." She managed a weak grin.

The officers left, heading down the walkway towards the gate. She closed the door behind her, sighed, and put her left land to her head. "Why did I say all of that?" They're bound to think she is hiding something—she is—but it's not what they're probably thinking.

The Prankster

The following day Fiona was busy at work, trying to keep her mind off of her brother-in-law's death. At least running the company helped her feel some sense of control. She sat at her desk, sipped Yasminea tea and looked through some drawings that a member of her creative team had presented her with. Occasionally, she'd swivel her chair around so that she could look out the window to gaze at the city skyline. The sun loomed high over the buildings, and shone down on their windows giving them the appearance of aurora borealis crystal. She always liked that view; Especially at Christmas time. It was evident to her why her father chose that location to set up his office where he could look down over the City Steel Tower and Oxford Plaza, in their shimmering splendor. Where he could enjoy the Holiday Light up Night from his office—and even let his family come in to enjoy the view. To watch the Fourth of July fireworks from his office was always such a treat in summer time. It was a shame he still wasn't there to share it with her. But she was grateful to him for everything, and gladly took up his place in the company, carrying on the legacy of *Etherwood Toys & Gifts.*

The intercom buzzed, interrupting her reminiscing. "Yes, Sheila?" Fiona asked, as she hit the button.

"Miss Etherwood," the secretary said, "You have two visitors."

This struck her as odd. She wasn't expecting anybody—and her sisters usually called before they came in. "Let them in."

The two detectives that she had met the other day came in, flashing their badges. Fiona was a little taken aback and frankly annoyed by their intrusion. "Hello detectives." She said, "What can I do for you?"

"Hello, Ms. Etherwood." Mulcahy said, "We're

just here to ask you a few questions if you're not too busy."

"All right, Gentlemen." She said, "Sit down please."

She gestured towards two wooden chairs sitting right across her desk. They sat down, looking around her office. "Nice Office." Mulcahy said, "Great view."

"Yeah, really nice!" Browning agreed.

"Thank you, detectives."

"Miss Etherwood," The older detective began, "we were just wondering—"

"Where I was on the night my brother-in-law died?" Fiona said, beating them to the punch, grinning at them as she sat with her hands folded in front of her. "I was here until Seven O'clock. Then I stopped at the grocery store on my way home. I went straight home and cooked dinner for me and my two younger sisters. Then, I went to bed." She shrugged.

"Did you know about the affairs?" Mulcahy asked.

"Know? I didn't know. Suspect? Yes." Fiona sighed. "He was never around. Always working with other 'clients'" At the mention of that last word, she wiggled two fingers of each hand up and down to indicate quotation marks.

"I'd always ask 'Maeve, why don't the two of you come to dinner tonight,' And she'd say, 'Reese can't make it…he's meeting with a 'client'…that sort of thing."

"Ah, I see." Mulcahy said.

"That rat fink!" Browning said, clenching his teeth. Mulcahy elbowed him.

Fiona smirked. "Well, she loved that rat fink, and she trusted him." She let out a sharp laugh then continued. "None of us could convince her not to. He could do no wrong in her eyes. No matter what we told her in regards to him, she would keep saying things like 'oh, he's just busy' or 'he'll be home soon' or 'he must be stuck in traffic'

"I think that she loved him so much, that she seriously believed that he was just as much in love with her, and that he'd do what was best for her. However..." Fiona let out a cold snicker and then shrugged.

"She was really *that naive?"* Mulcahy said.

"She loved him. She believed in him." Fiona answered, "Like I said, she thought he could do no wrong, and that he'd always do right by her." Fiona cleared her throat. She grew agitated. She didn't even like to think about Reese, about what he had done, and his untimely demise.

"Now, was this his first affair?" The detective pressed on with his questioning, despite her obvious discomfort.

"If there were more, I didn't know of them." Fiona said. "I can't prove anything. But his behavior was always consistent of a man having an affair."

"Did *your husband* have an affair too?" Browning chimed in.

"No." Fiona said, sharply. "No he didn't. Well, unless you consider that Vodka was his mistress. And he beat me. Often."

"Ah, I see." The young man responded with a nod.

"And, you weren't charged for his murder." Mulcahy said, not as a question but as a fact—a fact that he apparently had already researched extensively.

Fiona cringed and shifted in her chair. Her eyes met his as she spoke. "He was drunk behind the wheel of a car. He crashed into the telephone pole and died instantly. Nobody shoved vodka, whiskey, and beer down his throat. He did that all to himself—"

"Understood, Fiona." Mulcahy said. "Those kinds of accidents happen all the time. Too often, in fact. But two people in bed usually don't drop dead at the same time right in front of the wife. And, that's what we're—"

"I realize that." Fiona said. "However, I had nothing to do with their deaths either. In fact, I had very little to do with my brother-in-law at all."

"That seems to be a common consensus among you and your sisters." The detective continued, "As if you all thought your sister married beneath her status."

"Yes. She did. We both had." Fiona said, with self-assurance and confidence as if it was cannon, gospel fact. She stood, proud and regal. And, she did so commanding the detectives' respect. "My husband was a worthless drunk who, as it turned out, only loved me for my family's money. My sister's husband—a sleazy, opportunistic show biz lawyer—just wanted a trophy. A trophy that he could promote and show off...until a younger trophy came along. The jerk. He got what he deserved. Heck so did that singer-slash-actress!" Fiona was near tears, and turned to hide her face from the two men sitting in front of her. She couldn't stand to appear vulnerable and weak in front of them. Despite this, she sat back down in her chair, composed herself for a minute, and then looked at them with sincerity in her eyes. "But just because I feel that way doesn't mean I killed them."

"We understand," Browning said.

"Look, Fiona we're just trying to do our job." Mulcahy said, "Just trying to get to the bottom of this."

"I know that." She said.

"Well," Mulcahy said, as he got up from his chair. "That'll be all the questions we have for you now."

"We'll be in touch." Browning said.

"Okay, gentlemen." She said as she rose from her chair again and shaking their hands. She walked them to the door.

"Thank you for your time," Browning said.

They made their exit as she held the door open. Then she abruptly closed it behind them. Fiona leaned against it, sighing from relief. Her dark green eyes welled up with tears. She didn't mean to get so defensive, but they made her relive a painful memory, and she was full of mixed emotions now. She wondered if they could tell she was hiding something about Roger's death. And, if they could possibly think that it had anything to do with Reese? *How or why would they try to link these two very separate, very different deaths?* She wondered, *I guess it is because it's the second time in this family...*

Moments later, the intercom rang again. "What is it, Sheila?" She asked.

"Fiona, line one." The female voice said through the intercom, "It's Polly Rivera, Cayden's teacher."

"Gah!" She said, throwing up her hands. "Okay, thanks Sheila." She said, and then picked up the receiver. She put her head in her free hand. Cayden was obviously in trouble again.

🍃🍃🍃

Earlier that day Cayden sat in class, trying to concentrate on the book she was reading...

Then an unfriendly voice broke the silence, and aggravated her. "Her sister's a murderer!" Then, someone giggled. "She's going to go to jail, and that boyish spoiled brat is going to have to leave that big, fancy house and go in an orphanage. Haha!" It was unmistakably Patty Delani, who sat giggling with two other girls.

Cayden looked behind her at the skinny girl in her cheerleader outfit, and then smirked impishly. "Really?" Cayden snickered, "Well at least me and my sisters don't have elephant legs and a hippo butt! You'll have to leave your nice, small little house and move into a zoo!"

Sure enough, the chair collapsed under the weight of Patty who had blown up to four times her size. She got to her feet quickly; then screamed as she looked down at herself. "How did this happen? How did I gain so much weight so fast? I haven't even been eating a lot!" She stomped her feet, her arms flapped frantically.

"Miss Delani, calm down," Miss Rivera said as her kind expression turned grim with frustration and impatience. Cayden slumped down in her chair and buried her face in her book as she stifled laughter.

"I cannot calm down, look at me!" Patty said. "And there's a home game tonight!"

"OOH, talking back to the teacher!" Cayden taunted, "You'll get detention for sure."

"You spoiled witch!" Patty exclaimed, glaring at Cayden "It's not funny!"

"Oh, yes it is." Cayden said, "It's hysterical!" Most of other students were laughing, too. The rest just sat and watched, quietly amused.

"Miss Etherwood," the teacher said, "Don't instigate. You'll make matters worse."

"Sorry, Miss Rivera." Cayden said, with feigned politeness, "I didn't mean to annoy Miss Priss any further, as she's already in the middle of her hissy fit."

"YOU BITCH!!" Patty raged.

"Hey, don't call me by your mother's maiden name!" Cayden said, causing the other classmates to giggle. "Good one, Cayden!" her buddy Mitchell said.

"That does it!" Ms. Rivera ordered, "Both of you. To the principal's office. Now."

The classmates let out a collective "OOOOOH!"

🌿🌿🌿

"So what do you think, Barry?" Stan asked, as they drove out of the parking lot of Fiona's building.

"Me thinks the lady does protest too much," he replied. "She got a little overly defensive—especially when we brought up her own late husband."

"But that was a D.U.I. related accident." Stan reminded.

"Yeah, I know that. I just wanted to get her reaction. Test the waters a bit. It worked." Barry spoke matter-of-fact. He tried to hide his feelings of insecurity from his partner. In honesty, it didn't go quite the way he had planned. The Ice Princess was hiding something, and he knew it. She remained tight lipped, but he made her feel uneasy and vulnerable. "I was able to catch her off guard *at least*. If she had any guts to spill, she may have spilled it."

"So what now?" Stan asked.

"We watch and see what these girls do." Barret said, "They'll be nervous. Now Fiona may be innocent—but she's unglued. She knows something. She's going to go running and telling the one that is responsible for their deaths what happened."

"I still think you're barking up the wrong tree," Browning said, then nodded. "But I see your point. I see what you're getting at."

"What makes me suspicious," Barry said, "is that *none of them* attended their sister's performance—"

"Well Fiona did say she was working late." Stan said as he looked over his small tablet full of notes. "And, security staff at that building had already confirmed—"

"But," Barret interrupted. "What about the other two?"

"Well, the kid's not old enough to drive yet." Stan said. "She couldn't get there on her own."

Barret rolled his eyes. "No kidding," his sarcasm was unconcealed. "But, that other one, little miss attitude?"

"Well, she claims she wasn't feeling well and she didn't want to go if her brother-in-law was going to be there." Stan said.

Mulcahy countered with, "Yeah, but they all said he was never there for her anyways. And, it seems she hated Reese Warren the most."

"Well the other two can vouch for her being home." Browning said, "Can't they? Fiona did say that she made the girls dinner…"

"Hm," Barry said as he shook his head. "There's something very strange about these girls."

🌸🌸🌸

Fiona stormed into the school in a huff, her wings twitched as she fought to keep them well-hidden under her jacket.

"What did she do now?" She wondered aloud as she pushed through the door of the school and stormed down the hall. Her long, dark auburn hair blew behind her. She didn't need to deal with Cayden's reckless use of magic on top of everything else. "At age fifteen, you'd think she'd outgrow these childish pranks."

She reached the principal's office and walked right in, not bothering to knock. Cayden's shenanigans have made her pretty familiar with the principal and his secretary Marianne, who sat at her desk doing some paperwork. "Oh, Hello Fiona." They were now on a first name basis.

"Hi Marianne," She said, "Hello dear sister," She said, seeing Cayden stand up out of her chair.

"I was just laughing." Cayden said, "That's all. I wasn't doing anything real bad! I swear!"

"You can explain it to me later." Fiona said, as she signed a paper that Marianne laid out in front of her, which excused her little sister from school for the rest of that day.

"But I wasn't doing anything that bad," The girl persisted. "I was just laughing because she started being all prissy and crying around about being fat. I wasn't tormenting her."

"Suuure, you weren't." Fiona said, "Let's go. You can tell me all about it in the car."

"Have a nice day, Miss Smythe." Cayden said, smiling at the secretary, "I hope your cat feels better soon."

"Thanks, Cayden." Marianne said, "I'll see you tomorrow."

The two Etherwood sisters walked out of the building. Once she realized there were no more wingless people around Cayden started to grin mischievously. "All I did was wish upon her elephant legs and a hippo butt!" Cayden laughed, "She didn't literally have elephant legs and a hippo butt. They just blew up to the size of them! It was great! She whined like a baby about being fat!"

"Funny," Fiona said, with a smirk. "I suppose the little brat deserved it after all. But, you have got to be more careful, Cayden. What if you actually turned her into a hippo."

"Or elephant." Cayden said, still giggling.

"You could have exposed yourself as being a Faerie, Cayden. As being a magical being." Fiona's expression turned serious. "Do you want more reporters banging down our door than usual? Do you want to go through what Xandria went through with those pirates? Do you want scientist running experiments on us?" Fiona sighed, trying to remain calm, "You need to be careful, Cayden. What if something happened that couldn't be explained as something that occurs naturally or logically in this realm."

"But...but I didn't." Cayden said, "Anybody can gain weight at any time."

"But not that rapidly!" Fiona said.

"Well, in my own defense I noticed she had been getting a little chunky." She giggled, "I guess I just accelerated the process."

Now, Fiona couldn't help but snicker. "Just be careful, Cayden. Think about Maevis and what she's going through right now. Look at those detectives that keep snooping around. If they figure out that we're faeries, you know they're going to assume that they didn't just die of natural causes. They'll think she killed them with a spell." Fiona swallowed, recalling the death of her own husband.

"...And then it wouldn't take them long to figure out what *really* happened to Roger on the night you protected me from him."

"Oh, yeah," Cayden sighed. "Well, he was drunk behind the wheel. That stuff happens all the time." After all, there was still the possibility that he had died without any of magical intervention.

"Yes, however two healthy, young people do not just die of natural causes in the bed at the same time." Fiona sighed. Her heart raced as the sensation of panic rose within her. "I fear that that those detectives are going to figure out that their deaths are the work of a magical spell. If so, they're going to convict Maevis, *not even* understanding that she's sick and had no control...and then..." Fiona swallowed the lump rising in her throat, "Then they would deem us all dangerous. Our lives, for the most part, would be *over*."

"I see your point." Cayden said, as she hung her

head. "I completely understand now." Judging by the trembling of Cayden's lip, the uncharacteristic tear in the tomboy's eye, she understood all too well. Fiona didn't mean to frighten her; she just wanted her to understand the severity of the situation. This was no time for careless practical jokes against the ever-suspicious wingless.

An Upcoming Hearing

Maevis still couldn't remember what she said that night. What words did she whisper? Which spell did she cast? It was all a haze, as if she had been drunk at the time and was now suffering an extensive hang-over. She tried to recollect bits and pieces. The story had to be straightened out in her mind before the meeting with the Council. As she searched her memory, she also sorted through some things in her room: old pictures, one of their wedding invitations, some artifacts from her home world, her old dance memorabilia… Then, she found what she was looking for—a packet of seeds, in a tiny gold-toned silk satchel. She would use these later, to try to grow some Yasminea. Se felt that it would help to give her and her sisters strength, and sustain them in any worse case scenario. With the way things were going it was definitely a good idea to have their own little supply right outside the manor. *What if we're banned forever…?* She thought to herself, *Will this supply last long enough to sustain us? Will it even grow at all, in this non-magical realm?* She caressed the satchel in her hand, and was suddenly hit by a déjà vu.

An image flashed through her mind of the night in question. It was like a nightmare that she had woken up from, and only had the faintest images crossing her mind of that horrid evening. Of finding the man she loved and trusted in bed with another—in her bed. She remembered flying, wings unfurled…she remembered her belongings and a few of his flying across the room, like a tornado blowing through their home. The look of horror on that girls face as she screamed "She has wings!" as if Maevis was a monster. It only made the faerie more hurt, angrier…

Then Maevis' mind went blank. She cannot remember a thing after that, except for waking up and hearing her sisters call her name, Fiona shrieking…

They were dead.

He was dead.

She couldn't possibly have been the one to wish for this.

In fact, even in light of his betrayal she wished that he was still alive. And, that made her feel like a fool.

Oh, I should have known! She thought as she put her palm to her face, *I should have seen the signs. His negligence should have given me some indication. Late night meetings, lunches with clients, and how many performances he'd failed to attend. It doesn't matter now. He'll never see another ballet. He'll never be there again.*

"No, I'd never wish for this…" She said aloud, "This is not what I wanted. I would have asked him for a divorce, as well as severing all business ties with him—firing him as my lawyer and business manager. But death?"

She thought about it. If she had to cast a spell on him, it would have been to turn back the hands of time and make him the way he used to be; so affectionate and attentive. Not this distant, persistently absent man he had become. At worse, she'd have made him fall ill at the mere thought of another woman. But it was too late to think of that now. And, even faeries cannot reverse time.

There has to be a logical reason behind this. She thought. That same logic pushed away the fears that one of her sisters had done it—even inadvertently. *They disliked him and they thought he was negligent ant cruel. But murder?! They are not that vicious, and they were just as surprised as I was to find those two dead.*

In addition to that was the fact that none of her sisters new about the affair. "I should have picked up on it though," She whispered to herself as she clutched the satchel in her hand, "How could I have been so blind? Was I too into my own career to notice?" She began to cry, with her head in her hands. She recalled Fiona telling her that she was far to trusting with him. "She was so right."

"Maeve," a soft voice called out from behind her. She turned to see Xandria walk in the room.

"Maeve," Xandria said, "Are you all right?"

"You were right." Maevis sobbed, "I shouldn't have married him. I shouldn't have trusted him."

"Oh, Maeve, there was no way of knowing…" Xandria said, as she gave her sister a consoling hug.

"I was warned." Maevis said, "I shouldn't have married a wingless man."

"You couldn't have foreseen this." Xandria reassured, "None of us could. We're faeries, not prophets."

Suddenly the room grew cold, as another person entered the room. Dark gray and ghostly, she appeared in the corner near the dresser. "You're faeries, not prophets." Aunt Floraline said in a mocking voice. "How childish. How silly."

"What the hell are you doing here?" Xandy said, glaring at the old fae matron "You have nerve just showing up unannounced and uninvited. Maeve is grieving. She doesn't need you upsetting her further." Xandria spoke the truth—Maevis didn't need to hear 'I told you so' from anyone at a time like this; especially from Floraline. They all were fed up with their aunt and her domineering ways. Her imposing decrees and foreboding enchantments on the Gate, and all of her self-made rules since their Grandmother was too ill and feeble to oversee matters in Oberia. Xandria had assumed and even hoped that Floraline's stewardship of the kingdom would be only temporary. She and her sisters knew that had their father survived, he would have become King. But now, their grandmother had to name a new heir. They all feared she would pick Floraline, this coupled with the threat that they would someday be forever banished from Oberia. Maybe, she'd even ban them from the Hallow just outside Oberia's Gate—which would cut off their supply of Yasminea and thus cut off their lifeline. Without it they would be dead in a matter of months—the way their parents died. Xandy wouldn't stand for it. She would hold her ground.

"Well you'd now all about childish and silly. Don't you aunt Floraline?" The younger fae said, "You are the one who acted like a spoiled brat towards our father, whining that he was going to be King someday. If I didn't know any better…why…."

"Don't say it, Xandy." Maevis interceded, "don't give her the satisfaction."

Floraline stood over them, frowning on the girls with a stern look on her horse-like face framed with wavy gray hair the same color as her fly-like wings.

Xandy couldn't resist finishing the statement, "It's as if you wished my father dead! And my mother! If I didn't know better I'd blame you for the reason Maevis and I are so sick…next thing you know it will affect us all…Even Cayden. Poor little Cayden who's so innocent and never done a think to you. You witch!"

"Ooh, no." Her aunt countered, "That's your game, little child, not mine. That's your game of wishing people dead—even innocent, non-magical folk. That's something that you and your sisters seem to be very good at as of late. Mind you, your body count is growing." Floraline shot the two of them an evil grin. "But, then well leave that for the Council to decide on The Ides of March, at dawn. The council will see you there. If you fail to appear, you will all suffer the consequences. All four of you."

Her fly-like wings beat the air, three times. Then, with dramatic flair she left the room. "Good riddance!" Xandria screamed at the spot where her evil aunt as just standing minutes ago.

❦ ❦ ❦

Xandy stormed around the room, fists and teeth clenched in anger and frustration. "This situation really smells foul," She muttered. "And, so does Floraline as a matter of fact. She reeks like old, rotten cabbage."

With the Ides of March was only a few days away, there was little time to prepare for the Council. "There has to be something I can do."

The four sisters had to be ready to face the

accusations of the Council. They had to be strong. Maevis had a performance on the evening of the ides; but she would have to let her understudy dance in her place. Cayden hated meeting before the council, and Xandria did not blame her one little bit. They treated them both like children. And Xandria knew Cayden was stronger, and more powerful than all of their aunts put together—let alone the rest of the Faerie Council.

Xandria thought of her wicked aunt's snide remarks and haughty attitude, and a hand mirror flew across the room, and slammed into the wall. Xandy fought back against the feelings of dizziness and feverishness made worse by her feelings of anger. Even fear. Thoughts swirled through Xandria's mind. The police continued to snoop around the estate, arousing fears of Maevis winding up in prison. Her cruel aunt would love to banish them...until they suffered their parents' fate.

She tried to rationalize that fear away, muttering to herself "Well they cannot prove anything, can they?" Xandria tried to steady herself, hanging on to her night stand. The wings fluttered slightly as they draped over her back, the reflection in the mirror revealed a pale, faded version of her self. Dark circles loomed beneath glassy eyes. She fought against the sickness as she searched desperately for her necklace. Her hand felt the cool, sterling chain that held crystal orb that her grandmother had given her. The young Faerie slid it on over her head and felt an incredible surge of energy and strength. Whenever she worn it, she felt no malaise no and she was more in control of her spells.

As Xandria regained her strength, she continued to rationalize, "At least the police cannot prove anything. Circumstantial evidence..." She said to herself. "My sister found them in bed. She was devastated by his betrayal. Then she collapsed.

"What are they going to do? Claim that she's guilty of wishful thinking?" She sighed, as she realized that is exactly what Floraline would suggest to the Council. The old crone would claim that Maevis lost control of her powers, as a result of living in the

Outer Realm and that her rage had killed them both. Then, with no contest to the Throne, Floraline would claim it as her own.

"It is so like her to cash in on the misfortune of others." Xandy fought back against the feeling of utter despair. "Something has to be done. I need to talk to Grandmother."

Then, the young faerie changed into a dress suitable for her home world—a flowing green dress of gossamer and chiffon with velvet ribbon trim around the waist. She undid the messy ponytail that held up strawberry blonde hair and let her wings spread out over her back.

After she left a note for her sisters letting them know where she was going, Xandria headed out the door and through the back gate which led into the wooded area that bordered their street. Butterflies danced amongst the wildflowers, from blossom to blossom. It seemed as if they were greeting her. As Xandy walked on the path the forest grew dense, and the Estates of 15th street were completely hidden by trees. The sounds of woodland creatures drowned out all the nose of suburbia. Birds sang their songs to her, and far off you could hear the hooves of deer—or maybe it was the centaurs. After all, she was now deep into the woods where the habitants of Oberia and other realms were not afraid to tread. Xandria felt completely at ease, confident that even Floraline could not overpower her.

At last, Xandria reached the place in the woods known as The Hollow of Four Arches. Four pairs of tall, strong trees leaned into each other to form archways; their trunks intertwined into large trunk near the top. Xandria had passed through each of them. She loved to explore new realms, and experience adventures. Some of them were to uninhabited, desolate realms which made her miss her family. Other ventures were quite dangerous; like the trip into the Corithian Realm where she and a mermaid were kidnapped by pirates. Fortunately, with the help of her Grandmother's crystal, the two girls were able to combine their magical abilities and escape. The intermingling of their powers had a permanent effect on both of them. However, Xandria was also prone to nightmares of what happened on the pirate ship—of almost drowning, and nearly starving to death...

Needless to say, with all her adventures passing through the other Gates, she was happiest and safest in their own kingdom. Despite the fact that their father had more than adequately provided for them in the Outer Realm, Xandria always felt that she and her sisters were like roses amongst thorns. It was no secret that Xandria never felt that they belonged there. Oberia was home for the Faeries, and it always will be. With that in mind, she stood boldly in front of the Gate. Yasminea vines wrapped themselves around the arch of Oberia. Its full pink blossoms glistened in the sunlight that trickled down through the canopy of trees. Xandria inhaled its sweet odor which gave her even more strength. Her wings flickered and twitched as she walked through the gate. She smiled and looked around her, feeling comfortable and safe. Proudly, the young faerie walked down the path as it turned from dirt and gravel to smooth flagstone. Many faeries glanced at her and smiled as she strode past. Centaur minstrels galloped past. The sweet sounds of their harps, flutes and lyres filled the air. Giggling faerie children chased fire sprites in the fields. Xandria smiled, feeling confident and proud as she walked along the path that led to the castle.

As she reached the castle gate she smiled at the guard who seemed shocked to see her. His purple wings twitched as he exclaimed, "Lady Xandria!"

"Hello, Freydrich." She replied, "I am here to see Grandmother."

"But, but, my lady!" he began, seeming even more nervous and flustered. "Nobody just...comes right up to the door and asks to speak to the High Queen herself. It's against protocol! It's improper!"

Xandy put her hands on her hips, and tilted her head to one side. *Now, he's starting to sound just like his mother,* she thought. Her green eyes glared at him.

"But, she is my grandmother!" She said, "And last I checked, this place is just as much my home as it is yours, cousin."

It was true. Xandria was still a princess, even though her father chose to dwell in the non-magical realm beyond the gate. Despite the Queen's displeasure, she never renounced her son and his family, nor stripped them of royal privileges. It was as if she'd always expected them to come home. However, Penley's selfish sisters were very foreboding whenever he, his wife, or his daughters came back to Oberia. Floraline and Rosalea were usually unfriendly—and whenever they were cordial, it was feigned. Lylah was usually pleasant, but it was always in her hazy, dimwitted way. Xandria wondered if it was because of that organic substance found in the non-magical realm that she was so fond of smoking. It was weird, and it smelled really bad—and Lylah usually reeked of it. Somehow, the three aunts always managed to get in the way of meeting with Grandmother. Xandria was determined to see that it would not happen today.

"Hold on, I'll see what I can do..." Freydrich said.

"That would be fine." She said, "Thank you, Freydrich." He departed behind the door of the gate. Xandria waited patiently. Soon, he emerged again.

"Yes, My Lady." He said, smiling nervously. "The Queen's daughters have agreed to let you through. But..."

"You mean my aunts, my father's sisters." She said, boldly walking through the door. "No need to be so formal, Frey. I'm as much a part of this family as you are..."

"True indeed, dear cousin." He said as he managed to smile, and relax a bit. She strode in, slightly ahead of him.

Then, Xandria boldly walked into the throne room and pushed the door open. There they were, all three of them, in the room filled with candle light, marble floors and alabaster pillars. The scent of burning candles hung heavy in the air. Tapestries depicting various ancestral kings and queens hung on every wall. They sat on three brass thrones with red velvet cushions. Rosalea was a plump woman with strawberry blonde hair, streaked with gray. At her feet sat a fat, warty, sneering green goblin. The middle-aged princess narrowed her turquoise, beetle-shaped eyes and gasped when she saw Xandria enter.

Lylah however sat their grinning, dressed in a long cottony dress with bell sleeves—something she could have easily gotten away with wearing in the Outer realms, especially during the 1960's. Long, ash blonde braids fell at each side of her narrow face.

Floraline stood up, shot a stern glare at her niece and muttered "How dare you," under her breath. The undaunted Xandria smiled, despite the fact that she was around the most unpleasant faeries she'd ever had the displeasure of knowing—let alone Rosalea's pet goblin Chibito. The young girl was pleased to see that her very presence was unnerving to them; as was evident by the expression on their grim, holier-than-thou faces. After a moments silence, the princesses on their thrones just looked at each other. Then, Floraline spoke. "Well, Xandria. How dare you come in unannounced, just traipsing in past our guard. And how dare you let her, Freydrich. You both should be ashamed."

"Sorry Mum...I mean your highness," Frey said, bowing.

"Excuse me, I'm still family." Xandria said, "I assumed I was welcome. Besides, I'm not here to see you anyways. I'm here to see Grandma. It's urgent."

"Did you hear her?" The little, green goblin whined, as it looked up at Rosalea. "She thinks she be worthy of meeting Queen!"

"Yes, I heard her dear." Rosalea said, as if the thing were her daughter. "How shamefully bold! What an arrogant little brat!"

Xandy sneered at her. Her green eyes narrowing, she crossed her arms. *They are the ones being shameful and arrogant,* She thought. "She's my grandmother!" Xandria snapped, "I should be able to see her whenever I want. That goes for my sisters, as well."

"But...but...." Rosalea began, "You left our Realm—"

"You don't understand," Floraline interrupted, "She is the *High Queen!* Nobody just barges in to see The High Queen. Have you forgotten? Have you really spent so much time in that...*that place* that you forgot the rules that govern our society?"

Lylah just sat there, grinned, and nodded.

"I'm still a part of this family." Xandria said, "However long we have lived in the Outer Realm shouldn't matter. I'm here now and I expect to meet with my grandmother any time I want."

"Go away," The Goblin cried. "You don't belong here! You're not wanted here!"

Xandria snickered, "I'm more a part of this family than you are, you ugly little creature. Do you know that in the Outer Realm there are stories in which your kind is just innately evil and greedy?" She smirked, "Well, now I see why. I guess art imitates life."

"Don't speak to my pet that way!" Rosalea said. She cuddled the little green goblin as it crawled onto her lap. It cried, in a nasal high-pitched squeal. The sound made Xandria feel sick to her stomach.

"Ew. Shut that beast up!" Xandria said. "Anyhow, can I see my grandmother now, please?" She was growing impatient.

"Well, you cannot just barge in here and demand to see your grandmother!" Floraline said, "That's...well even if you are 'family' that's rude! And you're...you're just a..."

"Just a what?" Xandria countered.

"Just a child," Floraline said, shaking her head dismissively. "I'm nineteen years old!" Xandy said, "And, mind you, I've held private counsel with her when I was even younger than I am today; as did my sisters. For Heaven's sake, it was she who gave us permission to dwell in the Outer Realm even after my parents died—"

"Well, that was then my dear." Lylah spoke finally, "This is now. Your old grandma's not as well."

"And besides," Rosalea said. "You girls were warned! You were warned of what would happen if another wingless husband died. You were warned that you could be banished!"

"Only if we're found guilty," Xandy replied. "But none of us are responsible for their deaths, which is precisely what I want to see grandmother about."

"Well, darling niece." Floraline said, with condescending sarcasm. "This is simply not the time. Besides, this is completely against protocol." Floraline held her arms out wide, in her usual overly dramatic fashion. Her wings flapped to the beat of her words as if it was an uncontrollable tick.

"But this is an urgent matter," Xandria said, persisting in her efforts to meet with the Queen. "And, since it concerns her granddaughters I'm sure she'd want to hear—"

"Well, my mother is older now." Floraline said with feigned sympathy and phony sorrow. Her face cringed, as if she was trying to force a tear. "She's not in good health. She's...tsk...she cannot handle confrontation."

"I am not here to confront her or argue with her." Xandria said, "I am here to speak to her kindly, the way I always have! Have a friendly conversation and—"

"And, no doubt plead and beg for my mother to cast a spell that would make your trite little issues go away?" Rosalea chimed in as she rolled her beetle-like eyes. "Well, my mother is too sick to conjure up any kind of spell—even a simple wish—that would set things right for you four little twits!"

"For little twits!" the goblin echoed, followed with an evil nasal giggle. It reminded Xandria of an 8 year-old giggling at an obscene word heard at school.

Xandria let out a "Tsk!" as she put her hands on her hips, and glared at the grotesque little creature.

"Well, dearie, it *is* against custom." Lylah said, "But if you would like, I can speak to The Queen

Mummy, and ask if you can have a meeting with her at her earliest convenience." She grinned at her young, strong willed niece as if she had admired her courage. "That is customary, after all. Then, Xandy, I shall let you know when you can see our poor, ailing mother."

"Oh, thank you Aunt Lylah." Xandria said, "I appreciate your cooperation." Then, she glared at the other two aunts. "I'm glad that at least one of you is being considerate."

Lylah rose from her throne, still smiling hazily. She nodded to Xandy and then went through a back door that led through a hallway, and then to the Queen's personal chamber.

Floraline let out a nervous giggle, gave Xandy a fake smile, and then sat down. The aging princess wasn't doing a good job of hiding her displeasure— Xandria saw right through it.

Rosalea continued to coddle the goblin that played with her long, red and gray locks. Its skin nearly matched the color of Rosalea's green gown. "Careful, my Chibi," She said, cooing, "You'll knock the crown right off my head!"

Well, somebody ought to! Xandria thought. *Such a phony, vain witch! They're all phonies, actually.*

Her father was the only one who was never the type to put on airs, or to act pompous. She respected him even more now, seeing what kind of family he came from. He was humble, compassionate, and charitable; so very unlike his sisters.

She was also grateful that she and her sisters hadn't turned out like her coldhearted, selfish aunts. Xandria—like her father—always put others first. Like the mermaid she shared a necklace with, or the little girl who had her doll stolen in a playground when she was little. She wished the girl would have a brand new doll just like the one she lost…and so it appeared, right in the child's hands. Now, the young Fae stood patiently and hoped that her Grandmother would also be generous and benevolent.

After a moment or two, Lylah re-entered the throne room wearing a big, fake smile. "Sorry sweetie."

She said, "The Queen's not up for company today. You can come back in two days. She'll have rest by then. She'll be fine!"

"But, Lylah I need to see her today." Xandria protested, "Or at least before our meeting with the Council—"

"Don't worry about it." Lylah said, "She'll be well enough to see you in two days."

"This is urgent!" Xandria panicked, "And the council meeting is the following day. You cannot expect—"

"You heard my sister!" Floraline chimed in, "My mother will be well enough to see you in two days. You can wait that long, can't you?"

"Yeeeeeaaaah," The goblin jumped down from Rosalea's lap, and did a funny dance in front of Xandria. "Not like you're waiting for the lavatory, or you'll pee your pantaloons!"

"Shut up, goblin!" Xandria said, "You're so childish and crude!"

"Chibi, mind your place." Rosalea cooed, "some people are just not as amused by your humor." It laughed, crawled back over to Rosalea and sat at her feet.

"Fine then," Xandria nodded. At this point she was anxious to get away from the unpleasantness of their company, let alone that annoying goblin. "I will be back in two days to see my Grandmother. I will insist that you oblige me."

"Sure thing, dearie-dear." Lylah chirped. Head tilted to one side. "It's been a pleasure—almost. Give your sisters my love."

"Okay, Lylah. Thank you." Xandria replied, "I am glad to see at least one of you can be reasonable. I'll return on the fourteenth." Then, she turned to leave. As the other two aunts bid her a cold farewell Xandria exited the throne room.

As Xandy walked down the hallway that led to the door of the castle, she said "Well, that was almost eventful," to Freydrich.

"Nice try, my lady." He said, "It certainly took

a lot of courage standing up to them like that."

"Well, I needed to." She said, "Maevis is sick. I certainly needed to do something. I didn't want us to wind up banished. After all, well…that could mean the end of us. We'd suffer the same fate as my parents."

"And, I'd be sorry to see that happen, Xandria." He said, with sincerity. "And, none were more saddened to hear about the death of the Prince and dear Alannah than I."

"Thank you, your sentiments mean a lot Frey." She said, "You're family yourself, after all." Frey was Floraline's only son, though she never treated him as such since he refused to enter into a marriage she had arranged for him. She wanted her son to marry the daughter of a powerful political ally. But when Freydrich refused to marry the girl Floraline considered it a show of disrespect and ingratitude. She never fully forgave him. Ever since then, he can only stay in the palace as a servant rather than a member of the royal family. Hence he stood guard at the palace gate. Xandria found this shameful, and found their dispute rather trite—though she often wondered if there was more to it than that. "They're letting me come back in two days to see our grandmother," She sighed.

"I'm sure she'll be pleased to see you." Freydrich said, with a smile, "I really hope that she can help you. I'd hate to see you banished. But, I'm sure it would never come to that."

"I certainly hope you are right, Freydrich." Xandria said. "See you in two days."

"In two days, my lady." He said, with a sweeping bow.

With that, Xandria headed out the door as he closed and bolted it behind her. She headed down the pathway towards the Gate. Fewer onlookers stood around, though some children were still playing in the meadow catching fire sprites. Instead of the music of the centaurs she now heard the chirping of crickets. The sun was glowing orange, and easing its way behind the trees as Xandria headed back into the woods.

A Kind Stranger

As Xandria passed through the Gate the smell of Yasminea seemed even stronger. The blossoms that grew around the archway were and even brighter pink. She picked a couple knowing that Maevis would need them—and maybe she'd need a few for herself.

Then a voice called out from behind her. "Take as many as you want, my dear. More will grow tomorrow." Xandria turned to see a small, older woman in a long white cloak. Her face was concealed by the hood, which draped over it casting a veil of shadow. "Yes, I've seen to it that more will grow tomorrow."

"Well, um…that's wonderful. They look great! So healthy…" Xandria was quite amazed, and at the same time still curious about the stranger. She assumed that she was a wanderer, one of the Aelfen that roam through the bordering woodlands and travel through the Gates at will, seeking many adventures. Or, perhaps she was an old wise mage from the kingdom of Farlowen.

"You aren't well, are you?" The cloaked woman said, in a hoarse wispy voice. "So pale and thin, my lady. Well then, take them all. Share with your sisters. You'll all need your strength in the days ahead." Xandria could see a faint smile beneath the shadow of the white hood. "Like I said, more will grow tomorrow."

"Why thank you, kind lady." Xandria said as she plucked flower after flower, wondering how the lady knew about her sisters. *She must be some kind of mage,* Xandria pondered.

"You're quite welcome, dearest." The old woman said, "Now run along home. Maevis and Fiona are probably wondering what's keeping you."

"Ah, true." Xandria said, "Good-bye, then. But how do you know…"

"Farewell, my dear." The old·woman said. Then, she vanished through the dense trees. Xandria looked around, but the small white cloaked figure was nowhere to be seen.

It was getting late. So, Xandy ran back to down the path that led to the woods behind their manor. A bouquet full of Yasminea held firmly in her hand.

When Xandria came back into the house she was startled to find Maevis lying on the floor unconscious. She immediately took one of the blossoms that she was holding, and held it just below her sister's nose. "Come on, Maeve. Wake up." The scent made Maevis stir, but it didn't quite waken her. "Come on Maeve." She put the flower against her lips.

Maeve managed to open her lips slightly, and take a bite of petal. She soon came to, and whispered a faint "Thank...you." After swallowing the flower, she managed to sit up. "Where...where did you get them? Wow, they're so potent!"

"They were growing all over the gate." She said, "An old mage woman told me to take all of them. She said more will grow tomorrow."

"The archway Yasminea? But that's..." Maeve sighed, shaking her head. She knew full well that the Yasminea around the archway held special purpose for those who wandered out of the kingdom and should be used sparingly. "Let's hope she's right, since *we will* need it. After all, we could be cut off of the supply for the rest of—"

"Oh, Maeve, don't even think about it," She said, as she hugged her older sister, "Don't even worry about it. I have a plan. They're letting me talk to our Grandmother in two days."

"I don't know, Xandy." Maeve said, shaking her head, "None of us have been to see her since...well since a while! She's in declining health. I've heard she's very weak.

"Those horrible daughters of hers probably have her so brain-washed against us that it's not even funny! They're going to laugh when she tells you that she can do nothing to help us out of this disastrous mess."

"Well, hopefully she'll hear me out." Xandria said, lightly caressing the crystal orb that hung from a chain around her neck, "I've had a special bond with her, ever since I was sixteen."

"When she gave you the Crystals." Maevis managed to smile. Xandria helped her up onto the couch. Then, she sat next to her.

"Yes." She said as she touched her necklace, "The Crystals." She thought of how much it meant to her—and how strong and healthy she felt whenever she'd wear it. It really was special to her. It had even saved her life on occasion—especially from that horrid pirate. She gave the identical crystal to the Mermaid princess who was suffocating from lack of water, saving her life as well.

"Well, I certainly hope that Grandma remembers that." Maevis said, "They say her memory has been slipping."

"Oh?" Xandria said. Her smile faded. "Perhaps they cast some kind of horrid spell on her to make her forget all about us."

Maevis smirked, shaking her head. "Well hopefully the aunts are not that wicked…"

"Aunts?! They are no aunts of mine." Xandria ranted, "They weren't very good sisters to our father, either."

"Good point." Maevis nodded.

"They let him die, for heaven's sake!" Xandria was on her feet again, fists clenched. "They never even told him about how badly he and mother could fall ill from living in a realm void of magic. They finally told us about how Yasminea could sustain us when our parents were on their deathbed! They never cared about our father at all. Or our mother, or any of us!

"But, I'm still an Oberian citizen. I am Penley Etherwood's daughter; Queen Yolanda Etherwood's granddaughter. And, they cannot change that. Nor can they stop me from seeing grandmother, and appealing to her in regards to what happened to Reese."

"You go, girl!" Cayden said, as she came into

the door. "I hate those Bit—"

"Cayden!" Maevis said.

"Those witches!" Cayden sighed, and rolled her eyes.

"You really are picking up the local jargon around here, aren't you?" Xandria laughed.

Cayden's expression changed to one of concern. "Are you alright Maeve?" She asked. "You don't look well."

"She was passed out when I came home." Xandria said. "I had to give her Yasminea. She should be fine now. There's some sitting there if you need any." She nodded in the direction of the coffee table where she laid the flowers."

"Whoa, they're so bright!" Cayden said with a smile. "Where did you find them?"

"At the Gate," Xandy said.

"You mean *our Gate!?*" Cayden asked.

"Yeah, of course." She answered.

"Ah...?" Cayden was curious. "Why did you go there? Did you see Grandma?"

"Well I wanted to see her, and talk to her about Maevis, and what happened...and the upcoming meeting with the Council." Xandria rambled on, "However, I didn't get a chance to. Those spiteful shrews said she wasn't up for visitors today!" She shook her head, and muttered a curse under her breath.

"I dread the thoughts of that meeting." Maevis said, with her head in her hands. "They're going to say it was a wish-spell that killed them."

"Don't worry, Maevis." Cayden said, "There's no evidence. Nobody can prove you did anything. Not even our old miserable aunts."

❧ ❧ ❧

Barret Mulcahy and Stan Browning looked through the evidence spread out across the table. They had two wine glasses; one with lipstick around the rim. Two samples in vials of the wine from each glass. A plastic baggie containing some strange pink petals of a flower that oddly enough had not even started to wilt yet. Another baggie contained couple of tea bags found in the kitchen which smelled strangely enough like those petals.

In addition to all that was the typical evidence collected from crime scenes such as DNA samples, crime scene photos, and artifacts that could have been used as weapons. In this case that consisted of books, vases, cosmetics, brushes, and other pieces of debris that had been laying on the bed near the two bodies. Everything so far seemed inconclusive. They needed something concrete. There were no stab wounds on the bodies, no evidence of blunt-forced trauma, no bodily injuries. The current hypothesis was that the wife could have poisoned them. It was the only thing that made sense. Yet, it was getting harder and harder to prove.

"Look, Stan." Mulcahy said, "I know you like her. I know you want to believe—"

"Barry, she couldn't have been there in time to poison them." Stan replied, "She wasn't even home. You do realize that we have an entire audience full of witnesses, who can verify she was at the theater, don't you? Not to mention fellow dancers, choreographers, and everyone who worked back stage..."

"Well, it could have been a slow acting poison." Barret was getting impatient with his young partner. This happens often. Stan gets too infatuated with these young femme fatales. He would do anything to believe they are innocent; to prove his point. Then he becomes counter productive and it just about ruins the investigation. Normally, Stan is an excellent investigator. He's just too easily smitten, and so lonely. Barry and his wife have tried to fix Stan up, but it usually didn't work out for one reason or another. Stan would get too serious, and the girl would back off. Either that, or he had no interest in the girl and she called and bugged him all the time. Barret didn't mind Stan's occasional crushes, as long as it didn't interfere with the job. And, becoming infatuated with the main suspect in a double-murder investigation *is* getting in the way of finding out what exactly happened. *He just doesn't want to believe that miss Prima Ballerina with her long auburn hair and doe eyes could have done it,* Barry thought to himself. *True, she doesn't seem like a killer. True, she wasn't even home that night. She did seem shocked as hell that her hubby was having an affair. But that could have been an act.*

"What I find baffling," Barret said as he studied a document he held in his hand. "Is that Reese Warren had a life insurance policy out on the wife. Not the other way around. He could have been trying to kill her and run off with the bimbo, and then his plan backfired."

"Yes, drank the poison intended for Maevis." Stan said. "After all, look at the Etherwood house. Look at that toy company. He had more to gain from *her death,* than *she did* from his."

Barret nodded. "Unless it's revenge that she wanted. Or something else…the house?"

"It was in her name." Stan said, "Actually, everything was in her name." He shrugged.

Barret shook his head. His eyes roamed the table as if he was looking for something—expecting something to jump out at him.

"Those flowers!" Barret pointed at the baggie holding the petals, "They're the key. Take them down to the lab and have them analyze it. If they're toxic, well…at least we're on to *something.*"

"Alright, Barry." Stan said as he picked the plastic baggie up and headed out the door.

Barry sat there with his head in his hands. *There has to be more to this case than meets the eye.* He thought. *There's something we're missing.*

Unwelcome Visitors and Spying Eyes

Fiona gazed out the window as the sun began to set behind the city skyline. Her work day was coming to an end, and she looked forward to going home. Just then, a loud buzz came from the intercom on her desk. She walked over to it, and pushed the button. "What is it, Sheila?"

"You have a visitor, Fiona."

"Please, tell me it's not another police detective," She sighed.

"No," The woman's voice said over the intercom. "It's your aunt."

"Which aunt?" Fiona said.

The question was answered with the sing-songy "Helloo-hoo!" that chimed into the intercom.

"Okay, Lylah." She said. "You can come on it." Fiona sighed, and rolled her eyes. This was going to be unpleasant...but not quite as unpleasant as a visit from Floraline herself. Lylah would at least be kind, and mask her negative feelings behind her hippie persona and nature-girl flair. Her duplicity was like a Halloween costume that she donned all year round. And, though Fiona and her sisters never minded Lylah's company they didn't completely trust her; especially now that she had become Floraline's puppet. Fiona had the feeling that she was sent to do her bidding, once again.

The door swung open, and the gypsy-like fae stood in front of her, wearing a big toothy grin. Long, ash blonde braids were laced with silver-gray. She was wearing a tie-dyed smock and a long broomstick skirt. Her lime green tinted wings started to poke out from beneath the smock. "Hey, girlie!" She said, "Didn't think you'd mind a pop-in visit from your old auntie!"

As tempting as it was to say, "*You thought wrong*," Fiona opted simply ask "What brings you here?"

"Well…" The older faerie began. She tilted her head to one side. "Well, um…sweetie…"

Fiona braced herself. *Here it comes—the inconvenient favor that she always asks for at the most awkward times.*

"Um…got to ask you for this one little thing." Lylah said, behind a strained smile, as if she was constipated. "Sorry to ask but…"

"Yes?" Fiona wished she would just spit it out. She was getting impatient—and this was one visit that she had hoped to keep as brief as possible. She'd had a busy day and just wanted to wrap things up and go home. She couldn't bear her company as it was—and the smell of marihuana emitting from her aunt was quite nauseating.

"Um, well Xandria came to see us today." Lylah said, tilting her head slightly. "Did you know about that?"

"Yeah." Fiona replied. "Maevis said she left a note, telling us that she was going *home* for a little bit." She knew her aunts always hated when she or her sisters referred to Oberia, and specifically the castle, as home. So she made sure that she placed special emphasis on that word. Then, Fiona watched her aunt's smile fade.

"She did." Lylah began to look uncomfortable, and even agitated. "She wanted to see the Queen Mummy." She paused a minute. "Do you know why?"

"No, I don't, Lylah." Fiona said, sharply. "And why does that matter? She's our grandmother. We should be able to pay her a visit whenever we want. In fact, dear old auntie, as far as I'm concerned she has more of a right to show up at the castle and see grandmother than you do barging into my building to meet with me."

"But she's the Queen. And she's ill…she can't…she doesn't have as much strength as she used to." Lylah continued, again managing her fake, put-on smile, "I'd appreciate it if…um…we'd all appreciate if you didn't let her come back."

"No." Fiona said, calmly and self assured.

"She's a grown faerie, and she can do what she wishes. She has as much right to visit the castle as you do for that matter. And, more of a right than that ugly, ill-mannered goblin your sister keeps around! That thing is so…" Fiona cringed, "disgusting!"

"Yeah, she is rather gross." Lylah said, with a grimace that made he wrinkles in her face growing deeper. "But if you could…just…not let Xandy come back."

"You heard me. The answer is no." Fiona said, "As I said, she's our grandmother. And Xandy, Cayden, or any of us want to visit her we have that right. Don't we?"

"Well normally yes, but…" Lylah sighed. "See there's this thing…from the castle…and it's missing! I'm thinking if she comes back…well even more of the Queen's things might go missing, and—"

"WHAT!?" Fiona said, as she got to her feet. "Are you considering the idea that my sister may be a thief?"

"No dear," Lylah whined, "I'm only saying that…That I think she takes advantage of The Queen's good graces, at times. She expects my Mom to give her things, and—"

"Well, I've heard just about enough of this!" Fiona said, "This meeting is over. I'm busy. I don't need to deal with your pettiness. And as for Xandria's visits, she can visit our grandmother at will.

"You, however, were only let through because I told my employees that my family can come visit me whenever they wish. By family, I mean my sisters. *You and your sisters*—well you should have sent a messenger first. I'm busy. I have a toy company to run. I have every right to call my security team, and have somebody escort you out."

Lylah's expression turned to that of shock. She gasped. "You wouldn't do that to your auntie, would you?" Her wings furled out from behind her smock.

"Well, after what you've implied of my own sister, I certainly think I'm justified." Fiona gave her a satisfied grin. She hit the intercom, "Guards,"

The male voice called back "Yes, Ms. Etherwood."

Lylah huffed. With a furl of her green wings, she was gone.

Fiona giggled as she hit the button of the intercom. "Never mind, Reggie." She said, "She's gone now." Then, Fiona leaned back in her chair, and put her hands behind her head in satisfaction. "HA!"

🍂🍂🍂

The two detectives were on a stake out of Etherwood Manor, to monitor any suspicious activity. Barry Mulcahy yawned and rubbed his eyes. They were parked across the street, and behind some trees. A few glares from a neighbor with a beehive hairdo whose home they had parked in front of didn't bother them. They've dealt with worse. After about the fourth time the matron walked out to her car, or to get her paper, or to let the dog out, they actually found it funny.

She walked back in, and slammed the door. The officers snickered.

"Look, there she is!" Stan said, sounding anxious.

Mulcahy looked up to see Maevis, the oldest of the Etherwood sisters and their person of interest coming out a side entrance. She had gardening gloves on, and carried gardening tools and a small gold satchel. He got out his binoculars, and started observing her activity. *Not that a woman doing gardening is all that suspicious,* Barry though, *But you'd thing someone that rich would hire someone to do their gardening...especially a Ballerina.* Looking around at the landscaping, it looked immaculate as if it had been done professionally, "Maybe she's planting something that the gardeners don't know about." He said, "Something she doesn't want them to see." Last year, Barry had investigated a doctor who had tended one special part of his own garden to plant China White. The year before that, a society matron gave her landscaping team the day off so she could burry the evidence that she murdered her daughter-in-law. As Barry continued to observe her through the binoculars, he wondered if this could be one of those cases.

"Give me those!" Stan said, "Let me see."

"No way, Romeo." He replied, "No offense pal, but this is important to see what she does here…not to admire her beauty."

"Are you trying to tell me I can't do my job?" The younger officer said, in a tone indicative that he was offended.

"Not at all, Stan." Mulcahy said, reassuringly, "Just that…well I don't want you to get too distracted that's all."

Maevis Etherwood went over to a spot in the yard that was shaded by tall trees. A small, white fan-shaped trellis stood there. She started to dig with a spade, right at the base of that trellis. "Shouldn't flowers be planted in the sunlight? Why would she plant anything there…?" Mulcahy wondered aloud.

"Depends on the type of flower," Stan said. "Some of them need shade. Or so I've been told. My sister-in-law likes to plant flowers."

"Ah, I see." He said, "She might be a useful source of information…as soon as we find out what kind of petals we found at the crime scene."

They watched as the pretty redhead opened the small gold-toned pouch, and poured its contents into her hand. She then sprinkled them into the ground.

"Tiny, gold toned seeds." Barry said. "Write that down."

Stan jotted it down in a small notebook. They watched as Maevis planted the seeds, covered them up with dirt. Then she sat there for a moment, eyes closed. "Hm…looks like she's praying over them." Barry said, "Didn't think these richy-rich types were that religious."

Stan went to say something, but right at that moment his cell phone rang. "Stan Browning, here," he said. "Okay, gotcha. We'll be right in."

He hung up, closed the flip-styled phone and said. "That was the lab, the tox reports are in."

"Let's go." Barry said as he noticed the girl get up, brush herself off, and head back into the house. His car pulled out, and headed down the street. They noticed the nosy bee-hived woman glaring at them, through her window as they drove off.

Maevis walked back into the house and took a deep breath. She hoped that planting these Oberian seeds in the soil of a non-magical world would still produce healthy, full Yasminea blossoms. Even if they would be banned from their kingdom, they would have an ample supply of Yasminea right here at home.

After cleaning herself up in the powder room, Maevis went into the kitchen to make a cup of tea from the remaining Yasminea that Xandria brought home. She thought about Reese, and her eyes welled with tears. With all that had gone on, she hadn't had time to plan a decent memorial service for him. Sure, he was a lying, cheating snake. But, he was her husband and she loved him despite his betrayal. She stifled a sob as her frail, shaking hands ripped three iridescent pink petals from the blossom. She anxiously listened for the whistle of the tea kettle. The room began to spin, and her vision darkened. The tea kettle just couldn't boil fast enough for her. So, she put one of the petals in her mouth, and ate it. It helped to give her strength.

Then, when Maevis felt well enough, she sat down at her desk in the study and made plans for the memorial service. As she picked up the phone to dial the pastor at their neighborhood church she felt embarrassed to tell him that his body was still at the medical examiner, due to criminal investigation. "They're um…still trying to determine the cause of his death," She explained. "Yes, *hers too.*"

Maevis felt uncomfortable, like she was under everyone's microscope—not just the police. Apparently, the pastor knew some of the details of that evening already. After all, it was all over the papers, televised news coverage, and various local entertainment news shows.

"Oh no, Pastor Roberts." She said, "I don't mind at all. And I appreciate your kindness and understanding in this matter. It's been hard for me and my sisters."

She tapped a pencil, nervously, and then jotted down some information on a notepad. "Well, thank you very much Pastor Roberts. I'll talk to you then. Good-bye."

She hung up the phone, went out into the living room, then sat down and drank her tea. She decided to wait until Fiona got home to tell all three sisters about the memorial service.

❦ ❦ ❦

"Nothing?" Barret Mulcahy raved. "What do you mean nothing?"

"Just as I said," The skinny, young lab technician said. "And, the coroner's office said they didn't find anything in their system to indicate that the two were poisoned. There was nothing wrong with either of them physically. Both were in pretty good health."

"Yeah, I read the report." Barry said. He felt both skeptical and frustrated. "Is it possible that they just...were shocked? Scared to death when Wifey came into the room?"

"Well, that's one possibility." The tech said.

"What about those *flowers*?" Mulcahy persisted.

"Oh, that's what is really interesting." The tech began, moving over to the counter and examining it under the microscope. "Look at this!"

Mulcahy followed him, his forehead creased to the point his brows met in the center, he looked in the microscope. "Looks like glitter." He said, "Pinkish-gold glitter!"

Browning, who had been quiet up until then, took a peek as well. "Yes, glittery!" He said, "How bizarre."

"I've analyzed this compound and found this plant to be completely harmless. In fact, I've found it to do more good than harm." The tech continued. "The flower is a hybrid of sorts; A combination of hibiscus, rose, and jasmine. It's not toxic at all. In fact it seems to have healing properties."

"Huh," Barry said. "You don't say."

"It's like an herbal home remedy or something." The young man said as he moved over to a cage, where a large white rat scurried about. "This little guy was near death. Really dormant, we thought we were going to lose him. He's fine now."

"You're kidding!" Mulcahy replied. He rubbed his forehead, feeling like he was an episode of *The Twilight Zone*.

"Nope. I gave him a dose of the ground up flower, and he's fine." The lab tech said. Then, he smiled at the rodent. "Isn't that right, little guy."

"Hm." Mulcahy said, "Well, what exactly was wrong with him?"

"Some type of cancer, most likely." Barry and Stan just looked at each other—thinking the same thing; Thinking about his wife Marge.

An Army of Goblins

Floraline stormed around the throne room as her sisters sat in front of her. Rosalea seemed just as angry as she was, but Lylah who was high as a kite by now, was grinning despite her ire.

"Fiona wouldn't give in." Lylah said, "She said if her sister wants to come and see The Queen, no one should stop her."

"Hmm." Rosalea said as she scratched the ears of her little green goblin, as it sat upon her lap. "Interesting. Did you mention the crystals?"

"I told her we were looking for something that we think little Xandria has. She acted as if she didn't want to hear it. At all."

"I placed a gias! A Gias on the gate!" Floraline ranted, lines grew deeper in her aging face draped by long, gray wisps of hair. If not for her wings—which fluttered frantically—she'd look more like an old crone than a faerie. "And another spell on the castle entrance! Only if she has what we think she has in her possession would she be able to enter Oberia. Let alone, our ancestral castle."

"Not only that, my dear sister," Rosalea began. "You know what it means if she *does* have that Crystal in her possession!"

"Both of them!" Floraline raised her voice above that of her sister, so to dominate the conversation. "Both of the spare orbs were missing from the box! If she has one, and she passed another onto a sister…Do you realize what this means?"

"Yes…" Lylah tried to chime in, despite her dominant sister's control of the conversation.

"This means that *she* will be queen! *Those brats* will rule instead of us. Sit on our thrones." Floraline's voice grew louder and more emotional. "We worked so hard, fought so hard, and even broke a couple of cardinal rules in the process. We had to keep our brother at bay, whatever the cost, to claim what was ours!" She raised her fist in the air, "Yes, it ultimately cost him his death. Not that I feel guilty. It was he who chose to live in the Outer Realm, and do what he did, which expelled nearly all of his magical energies in that toy making scheme of his!"

She lent a moment to a dramatic pause. "Now, do you think I am going to let his daughters usurp us? I'll not have it, I tell you! I will not let them!" She flashed a cold smile. "If his child manages to pass through the gate tomorrow, we must stop her!" Floraline calmed, a minute. "She must not see Mother at all. That senile old bat would wind up turning over the whole kingdom to that little sprite!" She said the last word as if it was an insult. Floraline was notably prejudice against the other races and creatures in the kingdom, and only tolerated the Goblin Chibito for Rosalea's sake. Besides, since it often helped to do her sister's bidding, its services were about to come in handy.

"The creatures are ready?" Floraline asked with a venomous smile.

"We are ready, my future queen!" The Goblin said with a bow.

"They are prepared to head her off at the woods, and stop her at all costs." Rosalea answered. Then, laughed maniacally.

"Wonderful." Floraline said, with an equally diabolical smile, "And just remember to get that crystal! It must be mine!"

"Don't you mean *ours,*" Snapped Rosalea.

"Why yes, of course, dear sister." Flora said, nodding. "But mind you there are three. One for each of us. The one that Mother owns, the one that brat has, and the one that she most likely gave to one of her sisters. However, if I can get my hands on the one the brat has in her possession today, then I can set things in motion for the two of you to get the other two."

"But,...but..." Rosalea stammered, "Why should I let you—"

"Well, dear little sister," Floraline said, in a tone that was both condescending and threatening. "Have you already forgotten about our bargain? Or are you already contemplating your life in the Realm of Yogmore?"

Rosalea sighed, her skin turning pale white at the mention of that horrid place. "Agreed," she said begrudgingly.

Lylah just nodded.

"I shall rally the others, my highnesses," Chibito said as she departed the throne room. Rosalea smiled at the little creature as he scampered off--her closest ally in this deceitful plan.

☙ ☙ ☙

It was the morning of the memorial service. Xandria didn't really want to attend since didn't care much for her brother-in-law as it was. *Why should I pay any honor to the man who betrayed my sister?* She thought.

"Don't give me that look," Fiona said. "We need to support Maevis during this difficult time."

"But..." Xandria and Cayden said, simultaneously.

"No buts girls," Fiona sighed. "Besides, it would cast more suspicion on us if we don't show up at his memorial service."

"But they can't prove anything!" Cayden protested. "They just...died. And even if it was because of magic or a wish-spell gone wrong—which I doubt—those wingless detectives would have no clue. They don't even know we're faeries."

It was no secret that the two detectives had been following the activities of the sisters very closely, the past few days; even staking out across the street, in front of the Atkins' house.

"Cayden." Fiona said, "If you stay behind, that means you can't go outside and play basketball. And no going to the park with your buddies. All we need is nosy, old Mrs. Atkins nosing around, telling the cops what an irresponsible guardian I am *again*." She brushed her auburn bangs out of her eyes. "And,

Xandria..."

"Okay, I'll go." Xandria sighed, not masking her reluctance. "But, you know I cannot stay long. I *have to* see Grandmother. It might be the only chance I get to talk to her before we meet with the Council. I have to explain to her Maeve has been ill, and she wouldn't have had the strength to...."

"I understand, Xandy," Fiona said, "Of course I realize how important it is. Besides," She rolled her green eyes, "I'd hate to give into batty Aunt Lylah's request." Fiona tilted her head, and gave a toothy smile, "Well dearie, Do ya' think you could kinda...kinda not let her go. Queen Mom's sick you know...Not a good time." Her uncanny impression of their old aunt made Xandy and Cayden giggle.

"How about this..." Fiona continued, "Come with us and at least make an appearance. And then you can leave to see Grandmother."

Xandria smiled, "Sounds like a deal."

All four Etherwood sisters showed up at Oakhaven Community Church to pay their respects to a man who deserved very little of it—except, of course, in Maevis' eyes. She was his wife. Despite everything she loved him. After all, it was not she who had been unfaithful. Maevis had given so much of herself to make the marriage work, even though Reese Warren was an unfaithful, negligent husband. As Maeve sat there in the front pew images of that night swirled through her mind, making her dizzy and confused. She still could not recall everything about that evening. Just flashes. *Vases crashed into walls. Books flew off of shelves. Her wings propelled her over the bed. That girl screamed, "She has Wings! Wings, for God's sake!"*

Then, Maevis' mind went blank. She felt weak. Bouts of dizziness grew more frequent and lasted longer. Lately, cups of Yasminea tea could only give her strength for an hour or so. Maeve contemplated the need to return to Oberia to recuperate—at least for a little while. This made the threat of banishment even more horrifying. If the Council finds her guilty, it would be her death sentence.

At that thought, she glanced at Xandria. The poor girl looked nervous as she twirled her copper-blonde hair around her finger, bit her lip and repeatedly checked her watch. Maeve realized how restless and impatient she was and touched Xandy's arm. She whispered "You can go now. I know how important this is. Good luck, Xandria."

"Thank you, Maeve." Xandy said, as she hugged her.

Fiona reached over and hugged Xandy too. "Good luck, Godspeed!"

"I want go too!" Cayden said in a slightly louder whisper, "I want to help you!"

"Cayden, I'm fine with you coming along." Xandy replied, "But I don't think the *aunts* will allow it. Besides, Maevis needs your support more than I do."

A look crossed Cayden's face as if she had something else to say, but couldn't bring herself to say it. After a moment she said, "Okay, Good luck, be safe!" and gave her a hug. With that, Xandria quietly walked out of the Church.

Meanwhile, Detective Mulcahy's light brown Ford Focus was parked right outside. They spotted Xandria as she stepped out. "Oh look! Here comes that snotty one." He said, "Wonder where she's headed!" They decided to follow her.

Oblivious to their surveillance, Xandria walked briskly through the alley behind the church. It led to a pathway into the woods just beyond; which narrow, interwoven throughout the trees. She moved quickly, disappearing into the forest.

The detectives had to follow her on foot. They got out of the car and rushed down the alley and into the woods. The two men looked around but couldn't see her; it was as if she had completely vanished. Stan saw a flutter of pink flash by in the distance, the same shade as the girl's dress. He blinked, and then rubbed his eyes. "Over there," he whispered, "That must be her." The two men followed as best they could. They couldn't see the girl, but heard rustling through the brush up ahead and followed the sound.

Suddenly, a green, wart-covered creature about the size of a small hog ran out in front of them. "What the hell was that?" Barry said, as it ran off in the direction of the pink blur which they assumed was Xandria Etherwood. "Let's go!" Mulcahy said. They followed down the winding path; tried to keep up. The older, heavier man panted as he broke into a run. It seemed that even the younger, thinner Stan Browning could not catch up with the green creature or the Etherwood girl. Suddenly, another small, green being sped past. Then another. Then another...

"What are these things?" Stan said.

"I don't know...but I think" Barret heaved, "I think it's a safe bet that they're after the girl!"

"That's what I'm thinking." Stan said, "Do you think they'll hurt her? Do you think they're dangerous?"

"I think that it's a safe bet." Barry replied. "We better go, she may need our help."

Xandria stood still for a moment. Something did not feel right. As she sensed that someone was following her, she hastened her steps. Her furled wings twitched and fluttered, propelling her a little off the ground with each step as she ran.

There in the darkest, thickest part of the woods she could hear the stirring of small animals through the brush. They sounded as if they were getting closer. She could sense that they were forming a parameter around her. She panicked. Her heart raced. Xandy tried to peer through the leaves to see what was following her.

The detectives charged through the forest, down the path. Mulcahy was just a few feet behind Browning. Both men had their guns out of their holsters, in the event that they'd need to shoot the green beings. The strong scent of pine intermingled with pollen tingling in their nostrils. Stan stifled a sneeze. His eyes watered as he cursed his allergies under his breath. He had never been this deep in the forest before. The sun was completely hidden behind the dense canopy of various trees. He could barely see anything but dark green leaves. Then, he heard a scream followed by strange growling noises that grew louder and louder. "She's in trouble Barry." He said, "I can just sense it."

Xandria floated upward through the boughs. The creatures drew closer and closer. She peered through the overgrown foliage and bramble to see their snarling little warty faces. "Goblins," she gasped. "It figures!" They aimed their spears, tridents, and arrows at the Faerie. The goblins growled and grumbled as they shot at her. Xandria screamed from the pain as their weapons pierced and jabbed at her legs and feet. She didn't have much magical energy left—she had only taken a minimal amount of Yasminea that morning. She wasn't expecting any obstacles before she reached the Gate.

Xandy mustered up all the magic that she could, as she struggled to remain in flight. She was growing weaker. The arrows, spears and tridents continued to strike her. Then, suddenly she began to descend slowly. She tried to grab onto branches, to hold her self up. However, twigs would break off from the weight as she drifted downward. Downward, to where she would be at the mercy of those goblins. She managed to hold on to a pretty strong branch, clung to it as her wings twitched rapidly from fear.

Xandy had to do something. She summed up what little magical strength as she could. Wings fluttered. She started to drift up a little higher propelled by the frantic beating of her wings. She prayed for strength to fend them off. She started to chant a spell as she flew up higher. Radiant light shone around her. Wings flapped with renewed fervor. The faerie spoke in a voice unlike her own—ethereal yet powerful. However, the goblins seemed unafraid. Some shot arrows at the Faerie as she ascended. One nearly missed her wing. If it had hit it, and torn the fragile tissue she would have likely fallen victim to the army of goblins that seemed hell-bent on stopping her from reaching the Gate into Oberia. The faerie felt her energy drain. She grabbed onto a strong bough as she started to descend. Despite feeling weak, the faerie knew that she had to try again. She took a deep breath. Arrows flew past, threatening to knock her from the limb that she clung to. Then Xandria bellowed again, with a roar like that of a lion. Its crescendo echoed throughout the forest. The trees trembled, sending leaves tumbling towards the ground. They showered down on the startled goblins. Her roar grew louder and shook the massive trees themselves.

Finally, the goblins scattered. They rustled thorough the underbrush as they whimpered and sniveled.

And with that, all of Xandria's magical energies were depleted. The sickness overtook her. She let go of the branch and fell to the ground like a rag doll, weak and drained of energy. She plummeted to the ground, landing with a thud.

Moments earlier Mulcahy asked, "What was that?" in a hushed voice. "A bear?"

"Didn't sound like a bear to me," Stan said. "I think we ought to get out of here."

The men paused. The ground shook from the vibrato of the loud roar they had just heard. Leaves fell down around them.

Suddenly, they heard a strange scream, like a wounded animal. Soon, those strange green creatures came running past them in all directions. Some ran and hid behind rocks. Others crawled in hollowed logs.

One scampered about madly, and whimpered as it looked for refuge. It eyed the two officers warily and cried out "nyah!" Then, the goblin ran down a narrow path, deeper into the forest. It ran until a spot where streams of sunlight filtered down through the canopy.

There was no sign of the Etherwood girl, but they saw something truly bizarre. Eight trees paired off with trunks bowed into each other to form four archways. One of the arches was framed with flowers; the same flowers that they had found at the scene of the murder. Most likely the same flowers Maevis Etherwood had planted outside of her home the day before. The goblin scampered through that particular arch with fervor, As if it was running for its miserable life.

Xandria lay on the ground hidden behind trees as she tried to regain her bearings. "Bloody Goblins!" She muttered, weakly as she watched that little miscreant Chibito pas through the Gate. "No doubt who sent them after me."
She was however shocked to see two other people approaching the gate. "What are they doing here?" She said in a hushed voice, "They must have followed me." She recognized the two investigators. They looked shocked, and puzzled. She stayed well-hidden in the brush, watching them walk toward the gate shortly after Chibi passed through. "Uh-oh!" She said to herself, knowing that if they found out the truth about her family it would be disastrous. It was bad enough they suspected Maevis of killing those two people by some non-magical device despite the lack of forensic proof. But, if they found out that she and her sisters were Faeries, and possessed magical abilities then they'd naturally suspect that her magic had killed them. "No!" Xandria whispered, "Please don't go in!" she lacked the strength to cast the spell that would prevent them from entering her realm. Unable to bear the vision of two wingless people entering Oberia, she cringed and closed her eyes.

They two detectives looked at each other, nodded, and then slowly approached the gate. Suddenly a light shone from inside the arch. The flowers glittered pink and gold in its light. Suddenly, a strong force field pushed them back away from the gate, knocking them onto the ground. They two detectives looked at each other, nodded, and then slowly approached the gate. Suddenly a light shone from inside the arch. The flowers glittered pink and gold in its light. Then, a strong force field pushed them back away from the gate, knocking them onto the ground.

Xandria heard a WOOSH! Her eyes flew open. The gate glowed with pink-gold light. Yasminea blossoms glimmered like Christmas ornaments. The two men were tossed backward, landing flat on their backs. She grinned and sighed from relief.

"WHOA!" Barry said as he sat up, "Someone doesn't want us to enter that thing."

"Yeah," Stan replied as he picked his glasses up from the ground and wiped them off. "A little extreme don't you think? A simple 'no trespassing' sign would have sufficed."

"What the hell is this place?" Barry wondered, "What's going on here?"

As she watched the men dust themselves off and get to their feet Xandria remained hidden behind trees. Apprehensiveness about the men finding out whom they were—*what* they were—filled her mind and soul. What a three ring circus their lives would become if it was suspect that Faerie magic had killed the two people who were lying in that bed. Maevis got enough media attention as it was. And what would the humans do if they not only knew that they were Faeries, but considered that they were dangerous?! Xandria shuddered at the thought. It would be worse than last year, when she and that mermaid were kidnapped by a pirate Tragyn, mistreated and malnourished. He treated them like circus freaks, intent to sell them to the highest bidder that fancied mystical creatures. The experience was absolutely horrific. Thank God for her Grandmother's crystals that had increased their combined magic; and ultimately saved their lives. At that thought, she reached into her pocket and took out the precious heirloom. As she put it around her neck, she prayed it would give her the strength to reach the gate. The tingling feeling of restored energies surged through her body.

Then, Xandria watched the men walk back up the path, looking around. She'd need to get there quickly, and cast another spell...a spell that would make the men keep their silence about what they had just experienced.

As they walked of in the opposite direction Xandy emerged from her hiding place and headed through the gate herself. She passed through unharmed and unhindered. As she stood on the cobblestone pathway, she turned. She felt fresh, new magical energy surge through her. She whispered a spell.

"Hm. Weird." She heard Detective Browning say.

"I'll say," the older detective replied. "Hey, let's not tell anyone about this stuff...it's too...strange."

"Yeah, buddy." Stan replied, "I don't think they'd believe us anyways."

Xandria smiled to herself. Then, she turned and headed to the castle where she would meet with her Grandmother.

🍃🍃🍃

After the memorial service the girls emerged from Oakhaven Community Church to find the media waiting outside. Maevis looked pale, frail and tired as she hung onto Fiona's arm. Cayden was walking behind them. She was getting annoyed at the press which kept moving forward to ambush the girls, shoving microphones in their faces. Someone needed to do something, and Maeve was too weak. Fiona was always reluctant to use a spell in the presence of the wingless. Xandria was not back yet. *So I guess it's up to me, then.* Cayden thought as she took it upon herself to cast the spell that would make these reporters and photographers buzz off. After all, they clearly weren't listening to Fiona's request of "no comment."

"I wish you all would leave!" Cayden shouted and then whispered the words *"Trelijah, exodis iminea."* The reporters and photographers all backed off, instantly. She watched them retreat, hearing them murmur things like "Well I guess we're not going to get what we wanted," "At least we got a few pictures," and even "Come on, let's leave those girls alone."

Cayden grinned. Fiona turned and glanced at her with a look of amusement rather than anger. "Well hey," Cayden said with a grin. "At least I didn't turn them all into blimps this time!" She giggled.

"Yeah." Fiona replied, "at least this time you were more discreet."

Maevis looked worried, and inquired "Don't you think we should go find Xandria?"

"Well, let's give her some time." Fiona said. "If she's not home by sunset then we'll have reason to worry. But I know Xandria can hold her own against our aunts."

"Yeah, I know." Cayden said, as she wondered what was happening in Oberia at that moment. She was very curious about how long Xandy would be gone, as well as what their Grandmother had to say. Mostly, Cayden wondered whether or not Xandy would meet with any obstacles along the way. She could only imagine what her aunts would do to deter this visit. Cayden rolled her dark eyes at the though of it. She couldn't stand her aunts. Rosalea's impish goblin Chibito was just as bad; if not worse. When Cayden was little she and Chibito used to play games like hide and seek out in the forest. They'd even play harmless pranks on each other. But as Cayden grew older, she saw the true nature of the Goblin start to emerge in her childhood playmate. The pranks would become more cruel, and the games less fun. She would throw out wild accusations against Cayden and her cousin Freydrich. The goblin soon considered itself at home in the castle, acting as if it was a very prominent member of the family. It gained followers of its own kind due to its influence in matters of the kingdom. Rosalea did anything in her power to keep Chibito happy. Cayden often wondered if it was partially out of fear of retribution if she did not comply. Goblins were prone to be that way.

Barking up the Wrong Tree

"YOU HAVE FAILED!" Floraline said in her obnoxiously grandiose voice. She frowned upon the small goblin that sat sniveling at her feet.

"I am sorry my lady," Chibito whined. "We did our best!"

"Well I guess your best just wasn't good enough, was it?"

"Now, dear sister." Rosalea spoke up in defense of her favored pet, "Don't you think you're being a little too harsh on her? After all, she rounded up her fellow goblins to do *our bidding!* They *did* ambush the girl in the forest. At the very least, they managed to detain her for quite a bit. By the time she arrives Mother will already be resting, most likely. Or she'll be disappointed that the girl is late and think her careless. She may decide not to meet with her at all." Rosalea shrugged.

"Not likely!" Lylah interjected, shaking her head so that her braids flailed. "Queen Mummy's always had a soft spot in her old heart for little Xandy."

"True," Floraline said. "She has always made exceptions for her. And that is why I think she gave her what is rightfully ours. Those crystal Yasminea pendants!"

Floraline raised her hand and clenched it into a fist as if she was reaching out and to grab the necklace right off of her niece's neck. Floraline grinned, wickedly. Her fanglike teeth making her look monstrous, in that moment. The lust for power glowed in her grey eyes.

Rosalea stood up and held a hand out to her little goblin pet, as it ran to her feet. "Well, you did your best my pet," She consoled.

"I guess we've done all we could then." Lylah said, shrugging. "Just got to make sure we find her sister guilty tomorrow."

"Don't give up so soon, Lylah." Floraline said.

"Not like I don't have a few tricks left under my wing."

"Like what for example?" Rosalea asked.

"Just you watch and learn." said Floraline. "Freydrich! Come here!" She called out in a voice amplified by magical means. It echoed through the castle walls; caused draperies to billow. Candlelight flickered. "Freydrich, you are needed in the throne room now!"

After a few moments the lad appeared. "What is it mother?" He asked with a nervous smile. His royal blue wings twitched. Eyebrows rose up almost as high as his wispy black hair.

Rosalea rolled her turquoise eyes, "This ought to be good." She said. "Or not."

"Auntie Rose?" He mumbled. "What is going on?"

"Nothing dear," She replied with feigned kindness.

"Come here my son." Floraline said. The boy walked forward, and stood in front of hit mother. She whispered a spell. Then, the young man passed out cold; fell to the ground with a loud thump.

Lylah ran to his side, "Is he okay?"

"Oh, yes dear." Floraline said, "He's just sleeping, in a sense. He'll be awake within the hour. However, he won't remember what is about to happen." She flourished her arms, around like a figure eight with and muttered a spell. In a moment, she had transformed into an exact replica of her young son.

The two sisters gasped. Rosalea smirked and then nodded in approval. The goblin giggled, wickedly.

"Now if you don't mind, dear sisters," She said in a young masculine voice. "I'm off to guard the palace door!"

☙ ☙ ☙

Xandria headed to the castle, fully restored and feeling healthy. She inhaled deeply, relieved to be back magical atmosphere. With each breath she felt stronger, healthier, and more potent. Times like these made her wonder why her parents ever decided to live in the outer realm; why they ever put themselves at such risk. With that in mind, she feared what would happen if the Council found Maevis guilty. What would the punishment be, and would it extend to Xandria and her other two sisters? Would they dare exile them from Oberia? Or even from magical realms as a whole? "Yes they would," She said to herself aloud. "My aunts would be just that cruel." She looked down at her wounds—a reminder of that cruelty—and whispered a healing spell. The bleeding stopped; swelling went down. Puncture wounds vanished as skin meshed together, scar-free. Then, Xandria rushed toward the castle. She prayed she wasn't too late to meet with the Queen, and that delay hadn't offended her majesty. What if it was too late to meet with her at all? Tomorrow was the trail before the council. Timing was of the essence. Xandria felt like everything she had done—everything she was doing—was of the utmost importance. That their lives really did hang on the balance, and the result of this meeting would hold the key to the future for her and her sisters. It all depended on what the Queen said, what she believed to be true, and what she could possibly do to help them. Xandria hastened as she spotted somebody standing right ahead of her.

The strange, cloaked figure approached her again.

"Hello, dear girl." The White cloaked stranger said. "What is your hurry?"

"I need to see my grandmother!" Xandria said, "It's urgent! I am sorry, but I don't have much time to stand and talk."

The hooded head nodded, "Understood." She said, "But let me caution you for just a moment. Things may not be as they seem. People you thought you knew might not be who you think they are. *I* might not be who you seem to think I am, after all."

To Xandria's shock the old woman grabbed her hand and grinned mischievously from beneath the hood of the cloak. "Come with me dear. I have something to show you."

"But…but I can't…I…" Xandria began, "I have to see my grandmother. She's waiting for me. I had to arrange a special meeting, in order to meet with her!"

"Arrange for a special meeting, you say?" The old woman laughed, "One shouldn't need to schedule and appointment in order to see one's grandmother."

"Yes, I know. I shouldn't have had to." She tried to explain, as she rolled her eyes. "But it's a new protocol I guess. My aunts insist on making things difficult."

"Hm," The old woman said, "Strange indeed. Perhaps I can help you?"

"I don't see how." Xandria said, "Unless you can make me fly faster, right over the walls of the castle, and soar though the window into the Queen's own chamber?"

The lady gave her a funny grin, and laughed.

"Um…I didn't think so." Xandy said, "Well, nice talking to you but I really best be…Hey what are you doing?!"

The old lady tightened her grip on the young faerie's wrist, "Like I said, my dear, you must not trust that everyone is who you think they are. You must not take everything at face value. Your friends may be enemies, enemies your friends."

Then the lady held out her free hand which contained four small petals. Their hue was deeper than Yaminea's usual color; more violet than pink. "Here my dear." She said, "Take this. You will need it."

"Well thank you," Xandy said. "But, I'm home now, in Oberia. Surely my magic is strong enough here, and I don't need Yasminea to sustain me—"

"Take it!" The old lady ordered. "It's not Yasminea. They are Sharana petals. It will increase the magical energies within you, sharpen your senses. You'll see.

"Believe me. I know what lurks in the castle as we speak. Deceit. Lies. Trickery!" The old woman shook her head. Then she smiled again; a softer smile.

"You will have even more strength than your

darling little sister, if you take these. You will be able to face any adversary and trick the tricksters themselves. Beat them at their own game."

"Alright," Xandria said as she took the petals and eyed them warily. It seemed as if this old lady already knew what was going on. Who was she? A wandering soothsayer? Or just an old vagabond woman? Regardless, something told Xandy that she should listen to her. She put the petals in her mouth and ate them. Their taste was different than that of Yasminea, stronger and almost bitter. It reminded her of concord grapes. Right away, Xandria felt the glow of increasing strength. "But...who are you..."

Right as she asked the lady disappeared. Xandria's curiosity was peaked even more. *Who is she? How does she know what is going on, and why does she always turn up just at the right time?*

Xandria approached the castle with added strength and determination. She felt a new power growing within her. Wings fanned slowly in confidence. She walked up to the door, and was greeted right away by an unusually stern-looking Freydrich. "What are you doing here?" He asked, in a cold, unfriendly tone. "You and your sisters are not due until tomorrow."

"But Freydrich," She said. "Don't you remember? I'm supposed to see Grandmother today."

"Well," Freydrich said, "I just got word that the Queen is ill, and not up for *any* visitors. I cannot let you pass."

"But, she is expecting me." Xandria protested, "Remember?"

"No, sorry I do not!" He said, sounding unusually mean. "You can come back tomorrow if you wish. Maybe she'll visit with you and discuss whatever it is with you after the meeting...if you are still allowed in the kingdom, that is." He snickered.

Something seems very unusual about Freydrich, she thought to herself. *He's acting almost as nasty and condescending as his mother.* Xandria's wings twitched. An unusually sharp intuitiveness kicked in. She looked him in the eye and spoke the words, "Reveal your true self to me!"

Suddenly, he was transformed into his scowling, grey-haired mother. Just as the old crone raised her hand to cast a spell, Xandria exclaimed *"Trilijiah!"* Beams of yellow light emitted from the girl's hands. She pointed to her aunt. The light surrounded the old fae, encased and paralyzed her. Her face froze in a stunned expression as if she didn't expect the young girl to immobilize her so easily.

"You will let me through, as I wish." Xandria said, flourishing a hand towards the left. Floraline moved aside, without a will of her own. She shot her niece a haughty glare. Xandria strode on past her, giggling "Thank you auntie."

Barret Mulcahy and Stan Browning were waiting inside their vehicle as the other three girls arrived home. Neither of which said anything about the forest, those creatures, or that mysterious archway. They had hoped to see Xandria return safe and sound any minute—both embarrassed that they had lost sight of her and had not done anything to help her. *Whatever roared in the forest had scared off the greenies away, it had probably scared her off too...* Stan thought, "I just hope she's okay." He said aloud.

Barry shushed him. "Here they come..."

The Etherwoods did not do anything suspicious. They just got out of the car and walked right into the house using a side exit. Maevis looked even more weak and frail than usual. Dressed in black, with a black shawl around her shoulders; She leaned against Fiona as if she couldn't walk on her own. She was pale. Dark circles underscored her half-shut eyes. The youngest girl trailed a step or two behind, closing the door behind them as they entered. Then, Stan noticed the pink blossoms planted at the foot of the trellis were in full bloom already, growing in healthy vines that wrapped themselves around the white wooden fixture. "Look at those flowers," he said. "They sure grew, and bloomed up fast. Didn't they?"

"Yeah, I'll say." Mulcahy replied as he out of the car to take a closer look. "Sure did." He walked slowly, pushing the gate open. The ladies had forgotten to close it.

"Bud…watch out…they might see you." Stan said.

"I got to find out!" Mulcahy said, sounding urgent.

"Find out what, Barry?"

"Find out if it can help Margie." He said. "After what happened with that rat at the lab…I just got to know!"

"Oh," Stan said. He understood. Barry was looking for a miracle cure for his wife. "Well just…watch out!"

"Just think of it as collecting evidence!" He said, as he walked toward the trellis. Then, he looked around first to see if anybody was watching. The coast seemed fairly clear to him. Barry bent down to pick some of the flowers, shining pink and gold.

As soon as he touched one stem a voice called out, "Hello detective Mulcahy!" He jumped. "Hello, Miss Etherwood." He said, feeling both startled and embarrassed. Maevis stood there still clad in a black dress, wrapped in the black shawl. But she was standing on her own, looking refreshed and healthy. The pinkish tone had returned to her skin. Her green eyes shone brightly. She managed a slight smile. "Is there something I can help you with?"

"Um…I'm a little um …embarrassed to say this," He sighed, "But yeah, my wife is very sick with cancer. She's had chemo, surgery…and."

"Well, I'm sorry to hear that." She said as her smile faded.

"These flowers," He said. "It's rumored that they have healing properties?" He didn't know how to tell her how he found out. He couldn't bring himself to reveal his original suspicions of her. He failed to mention the crime lab results, or even the rodent that was healed by this strange plant.

"Oh, Yasminea?" She said, "Yes. In a matter of speaking, they do." She hesitated, "Um, here." She bent over them a minute, as if she was praying over them. Maevis plucked out five of the blossoms from the vine. Then, she gathered them in a little bouquet and pulled the blue ribbon out of her red hair, and tied it around them.

"Take these to her, set them by her bed. Let her breathe in their fragrance." She said, in a softer voice, "If that doesn't help then take a couple of petals, and make tea with them. She can drink that and it should help her feel better."

Barret took the flowers, and smiled. "Thank you Maevis." He said, "You are too kind."

"Oh, you're quite welcome." She said, "I hope she's better soon."

"Me too, miss." He said, "Me too."

Maevis nodded, and then headed back inside.

He got back in the car, looked at his partner and said, "You know...I'm starting to think you're right. We've been barking up the wrong tree."

"I told you." Stan said as he grinned.

"Yeah, now I understand what you see in her." Barry said, "Such a sweet lady. Completely harmless, and so are those flowers."

Stan nodded, smiled. "I'm glad you finally see—"

"The captain however," Barry said as he shook his head. "He's going to be a harder sell, and tell us to continue with the investigation. He still considers her our main person of interest."

"Even with no *real* evidence?" Stan cringed.

"Well, given the circumstances, and potential motive? Yeah." Barry said, "But if you ask me, the only thing she's guilty of is *maybe* a little wishful thinking."

The car drove off.

The Mirror of Dromenzia

Xandria Etherwood flung open the doors, and stormed into the candlelit throne room. "I demand to see my grandmother!" She said, "None of you can stop me!"

Unconscious Freydrich lay on a cot. Chibito growled at her, snarling. "How did you get past Floraline?"

"Like this little friend, *'Trelijah!*" The creature—less powerful than fae—was completely overcome, struck off its feet and thrown across the room. It landed on its wide bottom. Chibito sat there catatonic for a few moments, stunned.

Rosalea raised her hand, "Oh, no you don't....you!"

"*Trelijah,*" Xandria said again, overpowering her aunt, then "*Treshana...I wish...*"

"Don't you dare!" Rosalea said, with a nasty glare in her beetle-like eyes. She held up her hand, trying to counter the coming spell.

"You were frozen like ice," Xandria cast as a wish-spell, and her aunt was frozen solid right where she stood. Turquoise-tinted wings still. Arms still raised, face froze in a nasty sneer.

Right at that moment, Floraline came in after regaining her bearings. "How dare you!" Floraline's gray wings beat wildly; arms raised as if she was about to cast a spell on her niece. But, she was not quick enough.

"*Treshana!*" Xandy said, "You're frozen too!" Floraline, for once was still and silent. Xandria smiled, quite pleased with herself. The stranger was right. The Sharana petals made her even more powerful. She also had a heightened intuition; a sense of what was to come.

She took a few strides forward, daring her third aunt to stop her from seeing grandmother. She knew her tactics would be more subtle, and most likely covert. "No wait. Wait…and talk to me a minute first!" Lylah began. "I have something to tell you to um…show you before you see Queen Mummy."

"Sorry, Aunt Lylah." Xandria said. She could read her thoughts, thanks to the Sharana. She could tell that Lylah never intended on letting her see her Grandmother. "I'm not interested in hearing what you have to say." Xandria said as she walked unhindered across the throne room. She headed straight toward the large wooden door in the back of the room partially hidden behind a velvet curtain.

"We used to be so close, dear." Lylah said, with her head tilted. Smile bearing her horse teeth. "We use to be friends…"

"You ruined that, Lylah." Xandria said, "You ruined that by siding with *them*, against me and my family." Xandria pointed behind her, indicating the two frozen faeries.

"But, I'm family too!" Lylah whined, "We all are…"

"What a sorry excuse for a family," Xandria ranted. "When my parents were dying we trusted you to help us take care of them. You bided your time, and gave us the cure at the very last minute. How convenient your timing was. You waited it out just long enough to end their lives, before coming to us with Yasminea to look like a caring sister. *You knew* that it would be too late and they'd die anyways! Traitor!"

As Xandria turned towards the door, Lylah raised her hands and muttered *"Trelijah! Oceana!"* Right as Xandria opened the door a tidal wave rushed towards her.

Xandria held up her hand, palm out toward the tidal wave. It stopped before her as if she was standing behind a glass dam, changing its current. Then, she gestured with her arm in the opposite direction. With just that simple movement, Xandria reversed the water's flow so the wave burst forth towards Lylah. It swept her off her feet and carried her off with the force of its current.

Xandria grinned, "You forget, Lylah," She

called out to her aunt that was swept away, "that I have the power to wield water to my whim. Mermaid magic intermingled with my own. It saved my life, you know. Bye now, Auntie. I'm off to see grandmother." She strode through the door, shutting it behind her.

Xandria entered The Queen's chamber. It was much smaller and less ornate than she had expected. The room was furnished with a small canopy bed on one side, next to an elaborately carved wooden chair with a red velvet cushion and an equally decorative cherry wood vanity table.

Xandria moved across the room towards a large mirror with mother of pearl and sea shell framing. The mirror glowed with strange opalescent hues. As she stared into it, she did not see her own reflection but the image of her own house in the Outer Realm. She saw her sister Maevis talking to Detective Mulcahy. Maevis was gathering the Yasminea she had just planted into a bouquet and wrapping it with ribbon. Then, she handed it to the detective. "What the...?" Xandria wondered, out loud.

"So I see you've made it." A voice came from behind her, "I see my little tip helped." She turned around to find the white cloaked, stranger standing right behind her.

"What are you doing here?" Xandria said, "How did you get here?"

"Xandria Etherwood," the stranger said as if reprimanding her, "Didn't I tell you that people might not be who they appear to be."

The woman removed her cloak. She was petite, with an elfin face. Long, willowy waves of platinum hair cascaded down to her waist. She was wearing a pink velvet bell-sleeved gown. "Would you not even recognize your own grandmother?"

"Your highness!" Xandria said breathlessly, as she bowed.

"No need to be so formal, my sweet." She held out her arms to her granddaughter, who ran and gave her a hug.

"Oh, Grandma!" Xandria said, still holding her grandmother tight "It's so good to see you, finally!"

"They should have never kept you from me." The Queen said, "Any of you."

"They were so wrong." Xandria said, still gazing in the mirror, mesmerized.

"This is the mirror of Dromenzia." Grandmother explained, "It shows you important things that are happening at present, and things that have happened in the past. I suppose it's important that you see what you are seeing...your sister giving Yasminea to that man."

"I guess it must be," Xandria spoke as she tried to get around to the subject that she most wanted to discuss wit her Grandmother without seeming rude. "It's helping to derail their suspicions. But..."

"Can it reveal what happened on the night of your brother-in-law's death?" The grandmother said, as if she was reading her mind. "It surely can as soon as I figure out how, dear.

"You see, I'm not very familiar with the artifacts of Merfolk. It's rather alien to me. Perhaps a visit from my dear friend, King Dylyn, would be helpful."

"King Dylyn?" Xandria murmured, the name sounded familiar...

"Ah, yes, dear. This mirror was a gift from him." The queen grinned. "It has shown me many interesting things...I found out who you gave the other crystal to." Grandmother approached the mirror, and looked into it. She closed her eyes a minute, with a look of pure concentration upon her face. Then she opened her eyes again. The mirror reflected that of the Corithian Ocean from the Sirenian Realm; a place that Xandria had visited on one of her excursions.

As Xandria looked into the mirror she saw a young mermaid swimming toward a pearlescent castle. Her hair was as golden as her tail. "Aurelia!" Xandria said, as she recognized her. "If it were not for the crystal, and our combined energies, we would have never escaped that pirate ship alive."

"That's right." The Queen replied. "Look, she's still wearing your crystal. It is her Grandfather, King Dylyn that gave me this very mirror to thank me." The Queen turned and smiled at Xandria. "He really should be thanking you, dear. So when I pass from this world, this too shall be yours."

"Oh, I hope that day's a long ways off." Xandria sighed.

"Sadly, dear girl that day grows closer every day. Every hour. All of the wish-spells in the world cannot make me immortal. Nor shall I want them to. After all, a greater Kingdom awaits me than that which is here."

"Grandma, I need to ask you," Xandria began, "Do you think that you'll be able to see what happened before Maevis appears before the Council tomorrow?" There was a sense of urgency in her voice, and almost sense of begging. "Floraline and her sisters—your daughters—are determined to find her guilty at all costs. They're equally determined to convince the Council that what happened that night is worthy of banishment." The girl's lip trembled at that last word.

"Well, you need not concern yourself with that." The Queen said. "I've got it quite under control. Your old granny has a few tricks left under her wing." She winked. "And a few surprises that really should come as no surprise to some. There are things that have been set in motion for quite a while now. You see dear, I always new that my daughters would seek to usurp me. Fortunately, I've already named a successor."

"My father," Xandria said sadly, hanging her head. "Or at least it should have been him. He should have survived. Somebody should have done something to help them sooner."

"It's okay, Xandy." The grandmother said, as she gave Xandria a consoling hug. "I know you miss your parents. I miss them too. It's a good thing you have such wonderful sisters to take care of you."

"We all take care of each other," Xandy said. "That is why I'm here. To help Maevis."

"Don't worry, my dear girl," She said as

reached out a hand, and lightly touched the crystal pendant that hung from the silver chain around Xandria's neck. "There is nothing my daughters can do to stop what I have set in motion. Nothing."

Dusk set over the skyline of the city, and the hills just behind as Fiona gazed out the window of her office that evening. She had some work to do; things that just couldn't wait and had already been put off due to the death of her brother-in-law. She was dressed more casually than usual in jeans and a dark blue sweater; her long, dark auburn hair tied in a ponytail. She sipped her Yasminea tea, and surveyed the skyline again. She needed to come up with a new toy line for the summer—something that will outdo the competition. But more importantly, something that will bring children a lot of joy. That was always her father's motto. Penley believed all of the children, everywhere in the world deserved just as much happiness as his own faerie children; and he was intent to make even non-magical children's wishes come true. He never desired the riches of this Realm, but he wound up acquiring them anyways, and as he'd give them away to children's charities, and reinvest wealth into making more and more toys out of only quality materials…

As fate would have it, he'd just get more and more wealthy. His life really was proof that you get back what you give to others. Fiona promised him on his death bed that she would continue the good work that he began. She would abide by the same principals and virtues on which he built this great company.

She brushed her bangs out of her face, and sighed. She was having trouble concentrating on business…

As of late, no matter how hard she tried, she couldn't stop thinking about her sisters. Nor could she stop thinking about the death of Reese and that actress. She thought about what would happen if the Gate was closed to them forever. Their fate would be the same as that of their parents. Maevis had planted Yasminea which would keep them healthy for a while. *But if the flowers wither and die; or if we use them all up, and new ones don't grow up in their place...?* She pondered.

And, what of the local authorities, in this realm? The detectives surely feel that they have their rights to suspect us...just as they did when my husband Roger died. No, she had not wished him dead; and even if Cayden did it was well-masked from the eyes of any investigators involved in the case. He died drunk, behind the wheel of a car. In his back seat was a shotgun. He was planning on driving up to the estate, and shooting her. Cayden's timely wish-spell had saved her life. The accident was good timing, masking anything the wingless would find bizarre. Fiona had gone through an unbearable hell of a marriage. She was glad it was over, at last. But nightmares still filled her mind, in which she saw his face and felt the bruises that he had inflicted. She remembered the day she left him and all the stalking and the terrorizing that had followed. Finally, one day it ended. Ended in a horrific way—with a horrific realization—but it still ended. The cops questioned her when Roger died. But an auto accident with the driver full of alcohol? How can that be anybody's fault but his?

But this time it's different, Fiona thought. Two people of this realm—both in good physical health—died at the same time, in the bed just as the wife he betrayed walks in the door. *Someone has to protect Maevis. As weak as she was from the Sickness, even one day in a human jail deprived from not only magical atmosphere but Yasminea as well? That would kill her.*

Fiona regarded this, and felt that she had to do something. She may not have the strength to fight of the Council, and all of their combined magical powers. All of the Yasminea in the world couldn't give her that strength at this moment. She was tired and weak, beginning to show signs of the sickness herself. However, her pride would never let her admit that to anyone. She at least had power over those in this realm, and with that in mind she drank the rest of her Yasminea tea. She looked out her window over the city…and cast a wish-spell.

Night fell on the Etherwood estate. Moonlight shone on the trees bordering their lawn, just inside the wrought iron gates. Yasminea blossoms glistened on the trellis. Inside the large, white stone manor Maeve, Cayden and Xandria sat patiently, waiting for Fiona to come home. Xandria had shared with them the events that had happened that day in Oberia. They needed to come up with a strategy for the meeting with the council, and decide what they were going to say in their own defense.

Right at that moment a knock came on the door. Cayden rose to answer it, and walked from the living room to the foyer. "Why do I get the feeling this is bad news?" She said, as she approached the door. She opened it. "Uh-oh."

Detectives Barret Mulcahy and Stan Browning were standing in front of her with strange, shocked looks on their faces. "Cayden," Mulcahy said. "Can we please have a word with Maevis?"

"Okay," she said, "Come on in." They followed her into the living room. She feared the worse, and worried that they were really going to arrest Maevis this time. A lump rose in her throat. Her heart pounded. She escorted them into the living room, "Maeve, these two men want to talk to you again."

Barry smiled, "This won't take long, I promise." He said, "I…I just wanted to thank you."

"Thank me?" Maevis muttered. She was taken aback.

"Yeah, Um…" Barret continued, "The flowers you gave me yesterday. It's a miracle!" He said, "My wife…Margie…She sat up in bed, and talked to me like…like she wasn't sick at all! She was healthy!" Tears of joy were welling up in his eyes.

"That's great news!" Maevis said.

"Yeah, great!" Xandria said.

"I got so excited." The detective continued, "I called the doctor. He came to see her.   He wants her to go for some testing tomorrow…her heath seems to be improving. And I have you to thank, Maevis."   He shook her hand enthusiastically. "Thanks so much!"

"Also, there's something else we have to say." Browning spoke up, "We're declaring the deaths of your husband and Bambi Templeton a closed case."

"Yeah," Mulcahy said. "We have no reason to suspect you of anything involving their deaths. You're no longer a person of interest in the case. Your names been cleared."

"Thank you officers," Maevis said. She sighed of relief, putting her hand to her heart.

"Thank God!" Xandria said, as she put an arm around Maevis and hugged her.

"You ladies have been through a difficult time," Mulcahy said, "And, I'm sorry for your loss. Again, thank you for the flowers. They're like a miracle cure."

"Glad to hear that," Maevis said. "Um, Detective Mulcahy, if you don't mind my asking, what exactly did they find to be the cause of death?"

"Well, Maevis…strictly off the record," He said, "The coroner ruled their deaths as shock-induced. For both of them."

"Oh." she sighed. She had another flash of memory from that evening. Flying over their bed, wings unfurled. Objects flying…

Cayden said, "In other words, you scared them to death, with your—" Maevis glared at her, indicating that she should shut up before she says too much. Xandy elbowed Cayden. But, the detectives just laughed.

"Yeah, something like that." Barret said, "Good evening ladies."

"Goodnight, ladies" Stan echoed.

Then, both men left quietly, and closed the door behind them. Maevis let out a sigh of relief, and ran her hands through her bright red hair. She sat down on the couch, with her two younger sisters on either side. "It's over!" She sighed, "I mean, at least *this one problem* is over."

"Yeah," Cayden replied, "We've got those three witches to deal with tomorrow."

"Right," Xandria said. "But somehow I get the feeling they are the ones who are in for quite a shock. Grandmother was sympathetic towards us, and she sees what's going on. I think our old Aunties are going to be in for a surprise. Their old, ill mother is not so ill after all."

Right at that moment Fiona came home. Dark circles under her eyes. She stumbled in the door, and through the foyer. "Hi girls," She said, "Sorry I'm late."

"Fiona what's wrong?!" Xandria said, rising from the couch and running towards her.

"I just need Yasminea," Fiona whispered as she staggered forward.

Cayden grabbed some from a vase on the kitchen counter and then ran back into the living room. "Here you go."

Fiona took a bite out of a petal from a blossom.

"Oh, no!" Maevis said, "You're getting sick too?!"

"Well…" Fiona said, "Just slightly." She didn't want to worry them. They'd been through enough. And besides, Fiona was always too proud to admit that she was falling ill. She'd always been the strong one. She will always be strong for them.

"Well, rest up," Xandria said, "You'll need your strength for tomorrow."

"We all will." Maevis said, "I don't think the Council is going to be as convinced of our innocence as those two detectives were tonight." Xandria looked at Fiona, who sat recuperating on the couch. She seemed unsurprised by what Maevis had just said. She had the feeling that Grandmother wasn't the only one who had something up her sleeve, in the matters of clearing Maevis of all blame. She smiled at Fiona, knowingly.

The Ides of March

It was March 15th. Dawn rose over the trees as the four Etherwood sisters departed their house and headed into the Outer Woods that lay between their property and the Gate into their own realm. Their heads held high. None of which were afraid of what they would encounter in the morning meeting with the Faerie Council—especially Xandria. When they were a safe enough distance from the street, deep within the trees and hidden from prying human eyes, the girls let their wings unfurl to their full wingspan. Each girl was wearing a velvet and chiffon gown in colors complimentary to their wings. Streams of sunlight glowing orange through the trees, dancing in little specks on the ground as the wind blew softly. They were expecting anything as they trod through the woods. The goblin attack like the day before, or another enchantment placed over the Archway to their kingdom. Who new what to expect...? Every noise, every creature set them on their guard. Strangely enough, they reached the deepest part of the forest without any incident. Fiona sighed with relief. "Nobody stopping us yet." She said.

"Yeah, no Goblin Brigade." Xandria replied.

Maeve was quiet, just inhaling the air. She anticipated that the magical rush that would restore her once they got closer to Oberia. If they had come across a 'goblin brigade' she would not be strong enough to fight them off yet. Maevis felt that any creature that stood against them now should be so ashamed. Even if her spells had killed her husband and his girlfriend, it was nothing that she could have controlled. Any faerie authority can look at her, see how sick she has become, and determine that. Xandria seemed stronger than she'd seen her in days, and she was so proud of her. The way she stood up to her aunts, and insisted on meeting with the Grandmother before this trial was truly admirable. Fiona seemed to be regaining her strength since last night. Cayden was just as strong and confident as ever, dressed girlish for once in her dark gold, flowing gown. And, she seemed to be approaching this situation with a lot of maturity. So, in her sisters Maevis found new strength. With reassurance, she inhaled deeply and sensed the magic lingering in the air, as they approached the Hollow of the Four Gates.

Suddenly, the forest grew dark, and cold as grey, shadowy beings drifted out from behind a web-covered gate. They were the Banshees of the abandoned realm of Yogmore. The ghostly beings seemed to command the wind. They spoke in horrible shrieks and gasps, each face that of a horrifying woman. They say they are the ghosts of scorned women from Yogmore each wanting revenge for the deaths of their husbands that were lured to their death by Water Nymphs and Sirens. They swooped in and encircled the four faeries. "Wouldn't you know it!" Xandria said, stamping her foot. "The hags wouldn't leave well enough alone and let us enter unharmed, they have to summon the Banshees. It's like..." Xandria swatted at the ghosts as they floated toward her, "It's like they want to send a message, claiming we are just like them. But, we are not!"

"Trelijah, be gone demonesses of pain!" Fiona chanted, *"Be gone!"* Two of the Banshees shrieked, and then retreated back into their abysmal gate.

"Trelijah, retreat you wenches of darkness!" Xandria spoke, as three of them circled her. *"You have no power here, you belong to the darkness and I am a child of Light!"*

"Trelijah, Trelijah!" Maevis muttered faintly, barely audible as she fell on the ground. Two of the banshees encircled her. Their shrieking voices nearly piercing her eardrums. She staggered, trying to get to her feet. However, the banshees were relentless! They sensed her as the weakest one of their prey and drew in on her. They fed off of her pain. "Maevis, fallen who lost her mate..." One phantom cried, "You are the one to whom we relate...he was lured away, seduced just

like ours were that fateful day." The two continued their wicked, shrill song circling her, growing closer, "You know we feel your pain, young Maevis Fae…You want to seek revenge, and with us is your fate…."

"Join us. Join us…" they chanted. The other phantom-like beings joined in; swarmed around her to create a whirlwind around the weak, feeble faerie.

Maevis felt their jealousy, their rage, their strength as they sang. It seemed to drown her in despair. It made her feel the agony in her heart when she found Reese with that girl that night; reliving that pain over and over again. The image burned in her minds eye. The heartache completely overwhelmed her. As Maeve started to lose consciousness, she prayed that her sisters would be strong enough to fight them.

"Unlike you Banshees!" Fiona said, climbing up on a large boulder, "My sister still has love in her heart. Love for us! And she still has hope!"

"Fear, your sister has." Sang another banshee, "and fear we hold so dear."

"*Trelijah, you awful shrews!*" Xandria said, letting her wings carry her high into a tree. She stood on the same level as the highest flying banshee, "*I have the power. I am a daughter of Light! I am Granddaughter of the Oberian Queen!*"

"Your Queen has no power here," A banshee hissed as it flew toward her; cold breath blew on Xandria's face. "You shall drown in despair with your sister!"

"Not if I have anything to say about it!" Xandria said, and pulled out from under the neck of her gown the glowing, shimmering crystal with the Yasminea petal floating inside. It caught the light. She chanted a spell, and increased her strength. "*Trelisha!*" She chanted "*Flee!*"

Two banshees shrieked, and fled away back into their dark, spider-webbed gate. The four remaining wraiths hissed, and continued to circle their prey.

"*Trelijah, you evil banshees!*" Cayden cried, "*Be gone! You have no power here!*" She started to chant a spell, an orb of light shot out from her hands.

Then, jumped up and tossed it into the middle of the menacing, ghostly whirlwind that surrounded her oldest sister.

One of the smaller apparitions wailed and retreated back through the old, web-trimmed gate. The three sisters on the outside of the whirlwind flew high above the two remaining banshees now, "counter clockwise" Xandria said, "Let's beat them at their own game."

The faeries joined hands, circling the phantoms who circled the unconscious Maevis. A circle of light encompassed a circle of darkness. They whirled around in the opposite direction from the banshees, which broke the force of the whirlpool. *"Treshanah, evil spirits, you are done here."* Fiona ordered, *"Exodis iminea! Be gone!"*

The phantoms shrieked, fighting for control. But, the faeries' counter-whirlwind was stronger. Light shone on them through the trees giving them radiance that blinded the dark creatures. The light reflected off their wings and illuminated around them. Some of the banshees fled back into the old gate. Then, the last remaining one hissed "She is mine!"

"No she is not!" Xandria said, "Maevis is our sister. She's not like you! She's not bitter about what happened with her husband. She's sad because despite it all she still loved him. Even if he had survived that night my sister is not the type to seek revenge."

The banshee hissed, "You are so sure of this…?"

"Yes, I am. I know my sister." Xandria said, "Besides, in Oberia and even in the Outer Realm, not all women are like you. Not everyone blames other people for wars, famine, and misfortune…not everybody seeks revenge every time something goes wrong. Not all women want to kill the man who left her. We know about life or death. We lost our parents. She wouldn't have wanted to lose him too. *BE GONE!"*
And with that, the final banshee shrieked, and fled back into its old gate of rotting wood and a cobweb curtain. The winds died down Xandria sighed, and then looked

down at Maevis.

Cayden cradled her oldest in her arms. "She's going to be okay, right?"

"Sure, she is." Xandria said as knelt beside Maeve. She felt her wrist, making sure she could still feel a pulse. Then nodded, "Come on, Maevis. We've got to go."

Maevis opened her eyes, "I am sorry," she said. "I guess I'm just not strong enough."

"Maevis, I was barely strong enough to counter them myself," Fiona said, "Don't worry. They're gone now. We took care of them."

"No," Maevis murmured, "I'm not strong enough to go on."

"Come on Maevis, you have to!" Cayden said, "They need to see all four of us. If you're absent you'll be found guilty, and banished...and then you'll...you'll..."

"Cayden, I hate to tell you this honey," Maeve said, "Especially now, but I fear that I am dying anyways." Her voice trailed off, "I've felt it for some time now."

"Don't say that!" Cayden said, "Don't ever say that! We'll get to Oberia, and you'll regain your strength there. You'll be just fine." Tears were rolling down her face, by now. This tough, young girl who rarely cried was now weeping for fear of losing her oldest sister. "Come on, Maevis! You can make it!"

"I cannot, my...sisters." She sighed, "I am languishing here...it's as if fate has destined this. Don't worry...nobody will hold you guilty today..."

"We will carry you!" Fiona exclaimed, as her lip quivered. A strong, trembling tone lingered in her voice. "We won't let you die!"

"Here," Xandria said, "Wear this until we get there." She took the crystal from around her own neck, and put it around Maevis'. It will bring your strength back."

After a moment nothing happened. So, Xandria hung her head feeling like her effort was futile. She bit her lip, and questioned the value of the crystal. It seemed impotent in that moment. Then, Maevis opened her eyes a little wider and sat up a little, leaning against Cayden. Fiona sighed of relief and took Maevis' arm, helping her to stand up.

"Xandria," Maevis said, "You didn't have to give me this. It was sweet of you, but Grandmother entrusted it to you—"

"And she trusted me to do what is right," Xandria said, "And right now that is saving you. Come on, let's go. You can lean on us."

Maevis began to feel stronger as they approached the fourth Gate, the one trimmed in gold and pink Yasminea blossoms. As they stepped into the archway trumpets sounded. Two Centaurs flanked them on the path.

"Wow," Cayden said, "Why all the fanfare?"

"The Queen is naming her successor today," The Centaur guard on the right said, "She is passing the throne to her. It is time for her to step down. It is the Ides of March, after all." They sounded the trumpets again, and Cayden smiled. She looked at Xandria, who appeared a little taken by surprise.

She held her head high, and stood proudly. "Today of all days..." She whispered. "Wasn't quite expecting it so soon..."

"Yeah," Fiona said, "No wonder they sent the Banshees on us."

They strode down the path, uninhibited. No banshees, no goblins, nor any other obstacles got in their way. Their Centaur escorts flanked them the whole way to the palace gate. As they arrived, their kind-faced cousin Freydrich bowed. "Welcome home, my ladies!" He said to them as he held the door open for them.

The four young ladies walked in proudly. Maevis was feeling stronger, the color returning to her face. They entered the Council Meeting Room, where a large marble and wrought iron table stood in the center of 10 chairs of carved cherry wood. The Council members—including the three aunts—sat around it.

Chibito, now cowering and quivering, sat at Rosalea's feet. The other five Council members consisted of the Queen's two nephews, dukes Eurlin and Arils, Arlis' wife Priscela, Lylah's husband Ruffius, and of course the Queen herself. Her chair, for now, was empty.

"Come and sit down, foolish children," Floraline bellowed. "My mother is not feeling well, so she will not be here for the first part of our urgent meeting. The trial of Maevis Etherwood." Floraline cleared her throat. "The Queen shall only be present for the coronation. For now, I am still Quee...um," She cleared her throat again, "Chairperson of these proceedings. And, I say we get on with things straight away."

Maevis sat down, next to Fiona. Then, the two younger sisters sat on either side of them.

Floraline spoke again. "Maevis Etherwood, Daughter of my dear departed brother Penley, you are being tried for heresy. As well as the murder of two innocent, non-magical, wingless folk from the Outer Realm in which you dwell." The old fae glared at her niece. Her mouth distorted into an ugly frown. "How do you plea before the Council?"

"I am not guilty, chairwoman." Maevis said, proudly. "I have done nothing wrong that I'm aware of."

"But that is the key isn't it?" Floraline countered, "You were in a non-magical world. The very thing that killed your parents was dwelling in that Godforsaken realm beyond the forest for far too long." Members of the council began to nod. "You start to lose control of your magic when you get to a certain point in the illness, don't you? You start making things happen unintentionally...every little thing that crosses your mind becomes a spell, every little thing that you wish—every whim—becomes a wish-spell, doesn't it?"

"Yes but..." Maevis said, as her voice increased in pitch. "But I did not wish for this! I'd never wish him dead!"

"Ah, so you claim." Floraline said, "Perhaps you did in the recesses of your mind, out of anger and rage…finding *that wingless husband of yours,* in bed with that other *wingless thing!* Any woman would surely thing the most irrational, malevolent thoughts out of anger in such situations…why just look at…"

Xandria stood up, and Floraline shot her a glare. "Not my sister!" Xandria began, "She never would. We know that…and have always known it. In fact, twice this week I've seen proof of that!"

Rosalea rolled her bug-like turquoise eyes as the goblin let out a 'Nyet!"

"What?" Lylah said, rising at last, "What proof do you have to offer? What makes her so much better than the rest of us?"

"If she was like that at all," Xandria continued. "The Banshees would have claimed her heart and soul, and taken her off to Yogmore where she would become one of them. They ambushed us in the forest, on our way here. They attacked us less than an hour ago." Xandria glared at her aunts, "But go on, pretend you didn't know anything about that."

"Banshees!" An older, woman cloaked in white said as she entered the room, "Oh, not those dreadful souls!"

Xandria smiled as she recognized her grandmother, "Yes." She said, "Our Aunties sent us a surprising welcome party in the darkness of the Outer Woods."

The Queen pulled back her cloak, revealing herself to the rest of the group. "MOTHER!" Floraline said in disapproving tone, "I thought you were going to wait until after—"

"No need, Daughters." She said, "In fact, it's quite apparent that my granddaughters need me. I'm going to sit right here and oh yes, I'm definitely going to be involved in these proceedings. I have quite a bit to say, after all."

"Mother, sit down." Floraline persisted, "Be quiet."

"You are in no position to tell me what to do, Flora." The Queen said, "Last I checked, I was still the Queen."

"Well," Floraline said in a huff, "for now, anyways." She had an expression on her face as if the mother had tried to stab her. Then, she acted as if she had regained composure for a minute, however her fringed gray wings still twitching. "You mustn't believe them, Mother. You mustn't listen to what these silly, little girls have to say."

"No matter," The Queen continued, "I have all the knowledge I need thanks to my good friends from the Corithian Ocean. I have seen and heard enough to help me to pass judgment fairly and accordingly."

"Very well, Mother," Floraline said in a snippy tone, "But first we must proceed according to protocol. Each child must speak of the events on her own behalf, and then the Council must decide what their fate may be—if they be guilty or innocent."

"All right, then." The Queen said as she took the seat at the head of the marble table. "Proceed."

"We'll start with the youngest, then work our way to the one who is most likely guilty." Floraline said, shooting a daggered glare at Maevis. Then, she turned to Cayden with a fake smile. "Sweetheart, tell us where you were on the evening those two wingless people died."

"I've been there, done that." Cayden snapped, "We all know I was not at Maevis' home. I was shooting hoops at the playground." She cleared her throat, "I mean playing basketball. Then I came home, got cleaned up…" She shrugged, "Ate dinner. Went to bed."

"Well, then, tell us what you think happened," Barked Floraline.

"They died from doing the deed." Cayden said. Xandria stifled a snicker, "Died in bed. You know I have heard of weak-hearted wingless people having heart attacks during the act of sex. It's a no-brainer!"

"Yes, I'm aware that wingless are weaker than us faeries." Floraline said, in a huff, "But, it's no joking matter, is it?"

"No." Cayden said, "Of course not. But if they died because of that, then it's not Maevis' fault! They died of natural causes. And they got what they deserved."

"You say they got what they deserved?" Rosalea chimed in, "Just like you say that Fiona's husband got what he deserved—"

"Of course he did!" Cayden snapped. Her facial expression changed to one of bitterness, and maybe even shame. "I ...I didn't want him to hurt or kill Fiona! Ever again! Fiona takes care of me. She takes care of all of us. She's always been good to us." Her heart started to race, and she wondered if she had blurted out too much. Sweat formed on her brow and her wings began to twitch uncontrollably.

"Dear girl," Rosalea said, "We know what happened. I had figured it out all along. I don't blame you. I know what these putrid wingless humans are like...the evil that lies in their 'weak hearts' as you've said."

"You did again, didn't you?!" Lylah said as she pointed to Cayden, "You wished him dead? Just like you did with Roger?"

"You told your aunt a secret." Ruffius said, "And she confided it to me. You wished he was dead so he wouldn't kill your sister!"

"You wished your first brother-in-law dead, didn't you?" Floraline said, once again commanding the attention of everyone else in the room, "We all know that, since Lylah told us. So how are we supposed to believe that you would not be guilty of that a second time?"

Cayden shot a hurt, angry glance at Lylah. What she had confided to her years ago was in complete confidence; that confidence was now betrayed. "I was a little kid! I didn't know any better!" Hot bitter tears streamed down her rosy cheeks, her dark eyes now squinted. "I trusted you!"

"Oh, Cayden!" Fiona said, "Don't worry...I don't blame you..." She reached over and touched her sister's hand.

"I looked in his car...I saw a gun!" Cayden said, "I knew he was coming to kill you. I didn't wish him dead…I just said *'May he never hurt her again!'* My exact words! I swear on the Castle itself, those were my exact words!"

Rosalea gasped. The Council began to mutter as Cayden continued to rant, *"I NEVER WISHED ANYBODY WAS DEAD!"* Cayden's wings were flapping wildly as she levitated off her seat.

"SILENCE!" Floraline demanded, "Silence please!"

The commotion settled down, but only a little. Quiet murmurs brewed around the table. Cayden's face was flushed. She drifted back down into her chair as she tried to calm herself. Fiona took her hand, then hung her head.

"Xandria," Floraline said, changing focus to the second oldest sister. "You hated that brother-in-law of yours, as you hate all the wingless folk."

"I don't hate them." Xandria said, growing nervous. "I just don't care for them. I also felt that Maeve and Fiona shouldn't have married them."

"I agree." Floraline said, "I hope you girls now realize that no good can come from marrying those non-magical beings." She sighed, and then went on with her questioning. "You *hated him*, and so—"

"I did not *hate* him." Xandy protested, "I didn't care to be around him. And, I didn't trust him. That was all."

"So, you wanted him gone from your sister's life, I suppose?"

"Look," Xandria grew tired of the questions. She shifted in her chair, feeling agitated. "He was basically gone anyways. Never home. Never with her when she needed him."

"So did you and your siblings take it upon yourselves to um…spy on your brother-in-law?" Rosalea said, coyly.

"No." Xandria said, curtly. "None of us have the time to waste."

"So you say." Rosalea began, "But—"

Floraline interrupted. "You never went out to find out why? Where he was? Who he was with? Even though you were a Faerie with magical capabilities and able to find out all of that with just a wish-spell or chant?"

"No." Xandria said. "No, I never tried. I suppose I could have…maybe even *should have*." She sighed, and then continued. "But had I found out, I would have simply told Maevis. I'd have told her to divorce him. I would have never killed him. For heaven's sake, he wasn't worth the risk, or the waste of magical energy for that matter."

"Very well, Xandria." Floraline said, acting like her nieces' words in defending herself were irrelevant, unimportant, and practically unheard. Xandria crossed her arms, and huffed. *Oh, it's so like her!* She thought, *to ignore someone who makes a valid point, rather than admit that somebody other than herself is just or right about something.*

Floraline, after brushing off Xandria's words, was on to the next defendant. "Fiona, you are supposed to be so wise." She said sarcastically, "*Surely, you knew* of your brother in law's affair? Perhaps *you* wish them dead?" The old Fae allowed for a dramatic pause. "You have already gone through the same thing…more or less…an unsuitable, wingless husband. But *your* husband's mistress was *alcohol*." Floraline was so good at rubbing salt into an old wound.

"I knew Reese was up to something," Fiona said, calmly and coldly. "But I didn't know what or with whom." She shifted in her chair, clutching the arm rests. She did not need her husband's alcoholism brought up now. Especially, after the revelation that Cayden, at age 10, made a wish that saved her life. And, now it was coming back to haunt them. She hoped and prayed that her younger sister would see that they only exposed that detail—her big secret—to get leverage in this hearing. It was unfair, and absolutely hurtful of Lylah to betray Cayden's confidence.

"But do you think that Cayden would?" Floraline said, "After all, it has been proven that she is more than capable of committing wish-spell murder!"

"ENOUGH!" Fiona said, as she rose from her

seat. "We've just had enough of this! What Cayden did was nearly five years ago, she was just a little girl. And she didn't wish him *dead!* She wished that I would be safe. Incase you're too stupid to notice, there is a huge difference in that. She wished that he would stop beating me—she didn't suggest the method in which he would do so. Not at all."

"She is right, you know." The Grandmother interceded, "She is absolutely right."

"Tsk, oh Mother!" Floraline said, "What do you know about it?"

"Quite a bit, actually." The Queen grinned, "I saw it all in my mirror."

"What mirror?" Floraline whined. "What are you holding back from us mother?"

"Oh, you'll see dear." The Queen said, "You'll see."

"Fine then." Floraline sighed, and put her hand on her hips. Wings fluttered with fervor. "Let us continue then with the inquiry." She cleared her throat and gazed at Maevis with a haughty, condescending expression. "Well, finally we get to the main suspect in this...tragedy." She walked over to Maevis and looked straight in her eyes. The other three sisters shot their haggard, stern aunt dagger-eyes for her very demeanor and approach of their oldest sister.

"Maevis Etherwood of Oberia...you, of all people, miss dainty dancer..." She snorted. "You claim to have passed out in the middle of...something...you can't even remember what you said! And there are no witnesses there to verify your story. You *very well* could have said 'I wish thee dead,' and those two wingless, powerless fools would have died!"

Maevis tried to intercede, "I..."

"What can you possibly say to defend yourself when you don't even remember what happened that night?" Floraline ranted, not giving her a chance to speak, "Humph! You must have said it! You must have said 'I wish thee dead,' or spoke the killing spell of our own language to end their lives! Nobody else had…and you caught them together! It must have been you, in your jealousy and rage!"

"How dare you!" Maevis cried, as hot tears welled in her green eyes. "You dare accuse me of killing the man I loved! Even if I did wish something…or said something…it wouldn't have been *that!*"

"Well, dear, if you loved him that much, why did you take such a tantrum? Why did you do or say any spell…?"

"You condescending skank!" Cayden shouted boldly, starting to rise from her chair. With a stifled giggle, Fiona touched her arm, lightly, encouraging her to sit back down and not speak out at this time.

"I know what she said, and it wasn't a murdering spell." The Queen said, as she stood up holding the Mirror of Dromenzia. Xandria smiled, seeing that Grandmother indeed must have figured out how to use it to see things past…and possibly even in the future. Queen Yolanda ran her hand lightly over the mother-of-pearl and paua shell frame, and said, "Show us the day in question. Show us Maevis coming home."

Maevis saw the mirror image of herself in the garage getting out of the car, and running into the house. Hair was dripping wet. She remembered how she felt that day, feeling that something was wrong…

It was as if there had been a hidden video camera following her, tracing her every step through her own home. It showed her as she kicked off her shoes, hung up her rain coat, dropped her bag on the floor in the entry, and ran into the kitchen. The mirror revealed the expression on her face as she spotted the wine glasses.

Maevis felt a sour feeling in the pit of her stomach as she recalled how she felt that night. It was painful to relive the moment in her mind yet again.

"If only we could have shown this to the police," She heard Cayden whisper. Maeve watched herself stumble into the hallway, heard herself calling her husband's name. Maevis wanted to close her eyes, and to avoid seeing what would happen next. She did not want to relive that horrible moment. Yet, her eyes were fixated on the mirror. She watched herself and her reaction as she spotted the man she truly loved in bed with some hussy actress. She saw the shock and horror on her own face. Then watched her wings completely unfurl, and flutter with fury…elevating herself off the ground as she lost control of magic and a whirlwind began to spin around the room, all of their belongings, all of their objects….

"Trelijah!" She shouted, fluttered out into the hall uncontrollably, and there she dropped to the ground unconscious.

Moments later, the two people on the bed started to make this choking noise. They trembled on the bed as if they were having a seizure. The man Maevis loved was dying, and she was watching it…powerless to stop it. No wish-spell in the world could bring him back. Despite his infidelity, she loved him. She loved him still. A tear rolled down her cheek, as she watched the two people suddenly lay still on the bed pale as the banshees she'd been overtaken by hours ago. Maeve's heart beat fast and heavy within her, "I cannot take it anymore." She cried.

"Very well dear," The grandmother said, waving a hand across the frame once again, as the horrid image disappeared. "Trelijah. That's all my dear Granddaughter Maevis said. The overpowering spell. I've never known overpowering spells to kill anybody, or anything….unless it's accompanied by something else of course. And Maevis fell unconscious on the floor *before she could have said another word.* Even so, I don't think that killing would have been it. Just look at her! Even the thought of him dying is disturbing her!"

"Well then," Floraline began. "Who do you suppose it was?"

Rosalea, usually quite outspoken, didn't say a word. She sat, shifting in her chair, coddling her horrid pet. She could not raise her eyes to meet Maevis, who found this rather strange.

"I'll show you who…" The Queen said, with an

almost bitter tone to her voice as she stroked the frame of the mirror once more.

"AH!?" Cayden let out, as the comical image of Rosalea, out of her red and green robes and wearing a plaid suit that a wingless lady would wear if she was going to work in the office, fought to tuck her bright green wings into the jacket. She looked all awkward and clumsy. Her red and gray ringlets framing her face in a rather sloppy manner. As her surroundings came into focus, it was obvious she was in their own neighborhood; 12th street, to be precise. Chibi still followed her. "Okay, now Chibi, time for a disguise for you." She pointed a finger at her green, warty little friend, *"Transformeia!"* Then, Chibito turned into a cute little freckle-faced girl with blonde pigtails. She wore a red dress and black paten leather shoes. "WEEE! I'M PRETTY!" she squealed.

"Now, let's go my pet!" The matronly faerie said, grabbing the little girl's hand. "Her little abode is around her somewhere...She's the oldest after all. Surely, Maevis is the one who has the trinket from mother. Those little witches! How dare they take what is mine. Oh, trust me my Chibi, if I find this it won't matter that I'm second-oldest. If I find it before Floraline's plan comes into fruition then *I* shall be the one to reign."

They kept walking, eventually wandering down towards Maevis' home. "Hm...isn't that...that fellow looks familiar..." She spotted her niece's husband Reese Warren, helping the blonde Bambi Templeton out of the car. His arm was around her waist in an affectionate manner. Then, Reese kissed her on the lips. It was clearly more than just a friendly kiss.

Rosalea gasped. "Did you see this, my Chibi!" She said, "That worthless, wingless garbage cheating on a member of our Royal Family with that other worthless, wingless garbage!"

"Garbage! Garbage!" Chibito chanted. "Garbage man! Garbage man!" A woman walking past with an umbrella in hand, preparing for rain looked at the little girl and laughed. After all, Chibi's behavior was not unlike that of a mischievous child.

"Well, how dare he?!" Rosalea huffed, "I just hope Maevis doesn't have to see this rubbish!"

Chibito squealed, "GARBAGE!"

"Yes, My pet! They are garbage!" Rosalea's tantrum continued. "Hmph! Horrid, ungrateful, wingless human beings! *I hope that they both die in the bed that they lay upon together!"* Thunder roared overhead at her words, "Come now, Chibito." The old faerie said, "Let's get out of the rain."

Everyone in the council chamber gasped. The four young Etherwood sisters rose to their feet. "You!" Xandria exclaimed, "You all along! And you sat there acting all sanctimonious, pointing the finger at us!"

"It was you!" Maevis said, her voice trembling. Lower lip quivered. "You killed my husband! You killed the only man I ever loved!"

"But, he *was* cheating on you, dear." Rosalea said, "I was doing you a favor."

"Oh, a favor?!" Maevis said as white-hot tears of anger rolled down her cheeks. "Killing my husband and letting me and my sisters take the blame! I don't care what he had done…he didn't deserve death!"

"Yeah, he deserved for her to leave him and divorce him." Fiona spoke out, standing at her sister's side with her arms crossed. "Death is a little too extreme. And, for you to use this against us is just despicable."

Cayden arose now, her hand clenched in a fist. "I ought to—"

"Now ladies," The Grandmother spoke, "Let's all sit down. I have another announcement to make."

This seemed inappropriate of the Queen at a time like this, but Maeve didn't question her grandmother. Her heart still raced inside her chest as she wiped away the tears with her hand and tried her best to compose herself.

"I am officially stepping down as of today." The Faerie Queen said, "My successor has already been chosen. And she shall decide the punishment for Rosalea, as well as for the other two daughters."

"WHAT?!" Floraline said. Hands on her hips.

"Why us…?" Lylah asked, dazed and confused as usual.

"You were both culprits after the fact," the Grandmother said. "All three of you conspired in efforts to take over the throne for yourselves. Just watch." The Queen stroked the mirror's frame again.

This time it revealed Rosalea back in her regal gown, with wings spread out. Chibito was back in her natural form. They were with Floraline and Lylah in the throne room. "I was just paying her a little visit," She said. "I took Chibito with me, disguised her as a human child, and we headed toward her home…I saw her husband with another woman. That wingless *thing* that she lowered herself to marry was unfaithful! If you ask me, death was too good for him!" She crossed her arms, looking quite proud of herself.

"Oh, I agree," Floraline said as she grinned wickedly.

"Nobody can know about this!" Lylah said, shaking her head frantically. Braids flailed. "Nobody!"

"Nobody shall know. It will be our little secret," Floraline said, "Just like the secret that you told us about little Cayden. About her wish-spell on Fiona's drunkard husband. We can use these things to our advantage. We know that mother gave one of them the crystals."

"Yes," Rosalea said, "Question is which one?"

"It doesn't matter does it?" Floraline continued, "If they are found guilty of something as foul as wish-spell murdering two wingless husbands…well they'll be banished! I'll rule instead when mother passes!"

"What do you mean I?" Rosalea said.

"Oh, I mean *we* will rule." Floraline said, "We'll all rule together."

Impromptu Coronation

"I think I've seen quite enough, Grandmother." Maevis said, in a quivering voice. This conspiracy was all too horrific.

"All right, dear," The Queen said, waving her hand over the ornate frame one more time. It's time we move on to other matters. Ooh, Xandria I see you're not wearing the crystal I gave you..."

"Oh, sorry Grandmother," She said, bowing her head. "I gave it to Maevis. She needed its strength when we were facing the banshees."

"No worries dear," Grandmother said, "I knew you would do something like that again...just like you did with the Mermaid in the Sirenian Realm. You see, that young lady is the next to become Queen in her own kingdom thanks to you. That's why her Grandfather Dylyn gave me the mirror.

"However, I don't need a crystal to dictate who shall succeed me. I've known all along. You, Xandria, are the most unselfish person I have ever met. You always stand up for what is right no matter what the cost. And as we have seen, you put others needs above you own. Such qualities are worthy of a Queen of Oberia." The queen took off her own gold chain that held the crystal pendant. She walked over to Xandria, and then placed it around her neck. The girl held it in her fingers, studied it. It was even more beautiful, and slightly larger than the one she had just given to Maevis. Xandria stood up, smiling at her grandmother.

"Thank you," she said, with a small curtsey.

"And, let Maevis hold on to the one that you gave her. In doing so, you have already named your successor. A very worthy choice."

Maevis smiled, and said nothing. It was as if she was speechless to beseech such an honor. Fiona and Cayden looked at each other and smiled. Just then, Yolanda took off her tiara, pink gold with tiny opalescent crystals, and placed it on Xandria's head.

"My dear, I pass this crown to you. I trust that you will reign with wisdom, honor, and truth. And I trust that in your absence, Maevis will do the same. All hail Queen of Oberia!" The Grandmother bowed deeply.

Cayden and Fiona bowed as well, giggling from joy and relief. "All hail our queen!" Cayden said.

Lylah and her husband bowed timidly, as if they felt they were at her mercy. The rest of the council members bowed as well—except for Floraline and a petrified Rosalea.

"But…MOTHER!" Floraline ranted. Rosalea elbowed her, but she ignored it. "You said that you were not going to name your successor until after the trial verdict!" She clenched her fists, stomping like a child taking a tantrum.

"Exactly, my poor misguided daughter," The Grandmother began, "The trial of Maevis, Cayden, Xandria, and Fiona Etherwood is over. A new trial must be held to deal with," She glared at Rosalea, "the likes of you. I cannot very well set punishment for my daughters, can I? Even the thought of what you did disgusts me." She held up the mirror again, and one more time stroked the ornate frame.

It revealed Rosalea and the goblin still appearing as a little girl. Apparently, still the same day of the murder when Rosalea revealed the murder spell was cast by her, and their plot was revealed. The Yolanda's three daughters were deciding what to do next. "I guess that's what happens when you marry one of *them!* I …I just said it. I didn't realize how powerful it is when you wish on a whim…."

"They must not know!" Floraline said. "None of those girls must know, and most importantly our mother must not know!"

"Nobody will know!" Lylah said, shaking her head with vigor. "Just as nobody will know about what little Cayden did…oops! I wasn't supposed to say anything about the…about that!" She winced, and hung her head sheepishly.

"About what?" Rosalea said, "Spill it out, woman!"

Lylah sighed, "About the day that Fiona's human husband Roger died. Cayden came running to me! She was afraid it was all her fault. She wanted to ask me—since I am a member of the Council—if she could get in trouble. Now mind you, she didn't say that she wished he was dead like you did Rosalea. She said that she wished he would never harm her sister Fiona again. I told her it was fine. She can't get in trouble for that, and that it was probably was his own fault because he was very drunk."

"Well, well," Floraline bore a malicious grin, "This may be just what we need to help our cause." She paced around the throne room in her grey and green velvet gown. *Wings* flapped with vigor. "This could help us make sure that those girls never get to claim the throne. Especially that little brat Xandria! She's so close to our mother. I've banned them from coming to visit her. I placed a spell over the gate. None shall pass through it. That is, however unless they actually do have one of Mothers crystals orbs. We must find them. They must be ours."

"Very good idea, Floraline." Rosalea said.

"Well, now." Floraline continued, "All we have to do now is to implicate the sisters in both murders. That way, well they'll be banished! Penalized to the fullest extend of our laws!" She held her hand up in a fisted position, as if she was already declaring her victory over her brother's daughters.

"But...I...we..." Lylah tried to chime in.

"But. I. We. Nothing." Floraline continued to rave, "This is going to be easy compared to what we've already accomplished by putting our minds together. We let our poor, ailing deceased brother think that he could never come back. That he wouldn't be accepted again. This caused his death, did it not? He was the heir to the throne, and now he is gone because of our plan. Let us not forget Lylah, what a hand you yourself played in this with your own lies of omission. Thankfully, your little attack of guilty conscience in dealing with the situation—giving him and his children fresh Yasminea revealing that to be the key to sustain them—was too little too late. And, so it failed to prolong his miserable life. The poor, pathetic git that he was!"

"YOU BITCH!" Cayden shouted, as she turned away from the mirror to face her aunts. "LYLAH, I TRUSTED YOU! YOU BETRAYED ALL OF US! YOU WICKED SHREWS KILLED OUR PARENTS!" Fiona patted her sister's arm, trying to calm her down.

"Don't worry, sweetie. We'll get our turn to handle them." Fiona glared at her aunts. "They'll reap what they've sewn with this treachery."

"I think we have seen enough, don't you...?" The Grandmother said. Everyone in the room nodded; half of them from satisfaction; the other half from shame.

Then, Yolanda stroked the mirror's frame one more time. The images vanished. "It is for the new queen and her sisters to decide the fate of the women who hastened the death of their dear parents, and framed them for a murder that Rosalea herself had committed...all to seek the throne for themselves. Something that I am proud to admit would never have been theirs anyways.

"I gave Xandria two crystals for her 16th birthday, and have never regretted that decision. The crystals have the ability to enhance ones magical abilities, and to absorb new magic as well. Also, they signify that each owner is the next one to rule in their own realm. I knew that Xandy would be a wise choice, for her charitable and un-selfish nature. Also, Xandria is quite capable of making wise decisions and unafraid to confront any adversary.

"Therefore, Queen Xandria," Yolanda said, "You may now proceed with your rulings in this matter."

Xandria rose, feeling nervous. This was her first duty as Queen. She took a deep breath, and then spoke. "In light of what we had seen, and considering what my sisters and I went through these past few days...including the ghoulish attack on our way here today..." Xandria paused, wondering what action she should take. The retired queen nodded to her successor, indicating that she had bequeathed not only the crown to her but also her trust in this matter.

Queen Xandria realized that immediate action against the aunts would be prudent. Any delay would only give the aunts time to come up with another wicked scheme against her, her sisters, and even Grandmother. "And in light of what we just witnessed thanks to the mirror, I suggest we get to this matter immediately."

A Just Punishment

The meeting was moved to the throne room, at Xandria's request and her grandmother's recommendation. After all, this was no longer a matter of Council. It was up to the Queen herself, and Xandria was plenty angry at her aunts for all of their treachery.

She took center throne, which had been her grandmothers; formerly usurped by Floraline. At her request, Maevis sat next to her. Then, Fiona and Cayden took the seats on either side.

The Centaur guards flanked the thrones on each side, sounding trumpets as the four princesses arose. The prisoners—their aunts—filed in. The other members of the Council as well as Freydrich and Chibito stood in the back of the room quietly, waiting for the young Queen to speak.

"Okay, pardon my nervousness," She said, "I'm new at this queen thing." Some people giggled. However, her aunts just rolled their eyes.

"Rosalea Etherwood of Oberia, you have committed a sin against mortality by wishing death upon two wingless human beings. How do you plea, in this matter?"

"I'm um…well I know it's no use to declare myself innocent, thanks to mother's mirror." Rosalea began, stammering. Her voice sounded quiet and meek for once. "It was um…um an accident."

"But you tried to frame me and my sisters. You not only kept silent about what you had done—a horrible crime as it was—but you sat here in this very room and acted as if you suspected Maevis. Did you not?"

"Yes, I did but…but…" She pointed to Floraline, "*She* made me do it after all. You've seen her in that mirror telling us all what to do?"

"Yeah, you know I'd almost buy that excuse," Xandria countered, "If you were like that sniveling, half-witted creature that you keep as a pet. Bent on doing your master's bidding, no matter how nasty the task. But you have a mind of your own and can think for yourself, can't you? You're not her pet goblin on a leash!"

"Well true, but…" Rosalea whined, "You know what a domineering shrew my sister can be."

"I beg your pardon!" Floraline butted in as usual, full of her usual self-righteous indignation.

"Well it's true!" Rosalea said, "It always has to be your way, the way you want it, and we always have to follow your orders!"

"Silence!" Queen Xandria ordered, "Stop arguing like children! What does it matter anyways, neither one of you are in charge any more. Nor shall you ever be again. Remember, this is a trial to determine your guilt in the matter of the deaths of two wingless people; As well as the conspiracies between the three of you to frame my sister. Let alone the death of my parents." She cleared her throat, "So now without any further ado, I hereby pronounce you Rosalea Etherwood guilty of wish-spell murder of two non-magical beings, being careless and reckless with spells, and conspiring to conceal the truth. I also pronounce that you are now a fallen fae." Xandria held up her hand, whirled it around in a circular direction. And in an instant later, Rosalea appeared already ten years older than she was. Her red hair became ash gray. Her wings drooped, turning a pale, dull shade of bluish-gray. When a faerie becomes fallen, she is deprived of some of her magical abilities; it bears these visible signs. From the rear wall of the room, you could hear a low, hoarse growl of a goblin.

"And as for you, Floraline Etherwood," Xandria began to address the next subject.

"*Princess* Floraline Etherwood!" Floraline interrupted.

"My dear," The grandmother interceded, "You may be my daughter but you are no longer a princess. You gave up your right to that title when you conspired against my grandchildren; not to mention your hand in letting my son die."

"But…MOTHER!"

However, Yolanda disregarded Floraline, who stood there looking as if she'd been stabbed. The elderly Faerie Woman just nodded to Xandria and said, "Continue, my Queen."

"Floraline, you were the ringleader of this conspiracy." Xandria said, "You persuaded your sisters to keep silent regarding the illness of our parents, Penley and Alannah Etherwood. You let him think he could never come back; never told him that if they had come back to Oberia occasionally it would have preserved their lives.

"Furthermore, you never told them about the secret of Yasminea and its connection to our Realm and its magical atmosphere." Floraline tried to interrupt. However, Xandria continued, "You ordered Lylah to keep this secret from us! That is *murder*, as far as I am concerned!" Xandria fought to hold back tears welling up in her eyes, her voice trembling with a vengeful anger. The wound ran to deep within her heart.

"So what now?" Floraline said, her craggy face twisted into a horrid combination of anger, resentment, and haughty indignation, "Are you going to repay us an eye for an eye? Kill me the way you, in your paranoid piety, believe that I killed them?"

"We'll get to your punishment after all Three of you get your verdict." Xandria said, "You know the rules and policies as well as I do, surely. But for now, you are guilty. I pronounce you a fallen fae."

Then the young Queen held up her arm, and repeated the motion that she had done before. The older faerie's gray wings became darker, loosing their opalescence, drooping and looking more ragged around the edges as if she'd just walked through a thicket bush and torn them. Her face grew more gaunt and craggy than usual. Her eyes becoming a darker gray, just like the hair upon her head. "OOH," She whined, melodramatically. "Look what you've done to me! I do not deserve this!"

"On the contrary," Xandria said, "You really do.

"Finally, Auntie Lylah." The young Queen

proceeded, "You might be the worse of all. You weren't the wish-spell murderess, nor were you the leader in this conspiracy. But you were their puppet. You were their pawn, obeying them rather than listening to your own conscience. Your covert actions kept us in the dark, doing their bidding behind your hazy smile."

"But...but my kindness was sincere! I always liked you girls, you know that!" Lylah said, pleadingly.

"Yet you betrayed us." Xandria said, "You betrayed Cayden's confidence by revealing to your sisters that her wish for protection of Fiona may have resulted in Roger's death! Not only that, you used that as evidence against her in the proceedings earlier today! On top of all that, you withheld the truth that would have saved my parents' lives until it was too late to save them."

"Well, at least I tried." Lylah said, with her hands on her hips. "How was I supposed to know that it would be too late to save their lives? How was I supposed to know their health had declined so poorly that simply giving them each a Yasminea blossom wouldn't be enough to save them?"

Xandria disregarded Lylah's protest. "Therefore, I now pronounce even you, Auntie Lylah, a fallen faerie."

"NOOOO!" The vintage-clad faerie cried as her niece waved her hand in the air, in a circular motion one final time. The color of her wings faded pale, bland yellow and hung a little lower on her back. Her braided hair turned chalk white. Freckled skin turned pale, creased deeply around her eyes and mouth. The fallen faeries crowded together embracing.

The young Queen spoke, "I shall now give you the verdict. After what my sisters and I have gone through I sentence you to exile in Yogmore, forever to deal with those insufferable Banshees that you sprung upon us this morning."

The three aunts' frowns grew deeper. Rosalea let out a loud, moan. "Won't you show your old aunts some mercy?" Floraline begged, "At least for the sake of family?"

"Family?" Xandria said, "You should have thought about that when you let my parents die, framed Maevis, sent goblins and ghosts upon us..." She shook her head, in disgust. Then, without further ado Xandria ordered, "Guards. Please take them away. Take them to the gate at Yogmore. Cast the spell to prevent them from ever leaving its web-covered gate."

"Of course, your majesty." The centaur said. The guards walked to the fallen sisters, bound their hands with rope, and escorted them out of the castle. Behind them, the sniveling goblin Chibito scurried out the door, crying "Nyeeet!"

"Well done, your majesty." Fiona said, smiling. "That was precisely what they deserved. Hm. I think it is time for a change in this old place." With a wave of her hand, the room became filled with candles and lanterns that gave off glorious white light. And vases full of flowers, not to mention tapestries showing only happy scenes from when the kingdom was more jubilant; As well as portraits of Penley, Alannah, and their four beautiful daughters.

"The members of the Council shall be appointed as follows," Xandria said. "Of course I, as Queen shall sit as the head of Council. Agreed!"

"Agreed!" All of the people in the throne room said in unison.

"I shall now appoint my three sisters to sit with me on the council: Fiona, Maevis and Cayden. I'd like to include our cousin, Freydrich. Are we all in agreement on that?" Xandria smiled at her sisters.

"Agreed!" Everyone echoed.

"It's settled then." Xandria said, "And this marks a new day in Oberia. From now on Faerie kind shall not suffer the likes of those three—who plotted against their own brother, and his wife and children."

"Yeah," Cayden interjected. "No more Banshee ambushes and evil little goblins doing their bidding."

"Oh, of course not." Xandria said. "Who could possibly expect peace and harmony with beings like those—especially the banshees. They thrive on pain, misery, envy and hate."

"Ew." Cayden said.

"Yeah, I know." Xandria said, "Only the most evil, treacherous faerie would ever form allegiance with them and use them to attack their own family."

"Well they are gone now," Maevis said, "There is no reason to fear from them and their deceit any more. It is done. And you, my darling sister Xandria, are the queen." Maevis smiled. Nothing could daunt her joy at seeing her young sister where she truly belongs. Xandria was just beaming, more content than she had ever been in her whole life.

"Fiona," Xandria said as she turned to her older sister. "I understand if you wish to go back to the Outer Realm and continue to run the toy company. You are free to do so. But please know that you are always welcome here. It is your home too, after all."

Fiona smiled. This was something that truly made her happy. "Oh, that's ideal!" She said. "I'm sure I'll need to come and get some rest and restore my energies…especially after Christmas time."

"And, if it's okay with you Xandy," Cayden asked, "Can I stay with Fiona in the Outer Realm too? So, I can still hang out with Mitch and play basketball?"

"Of course, Cayden." Xandria said, smiling at her. "But please know, you're allowed to play here too. Maybe you and Freydrich can organize a team."

The sisters laughed.

"As for me," Maevis said, softly and timidly, "I'd like to stay *here* with you. I feel I am too ill to continue living in the Outer Realm. And, Lord knows, at Thirty-two it's about time I retired from dancing. Give these younger ballerinas a time to shine. My time is gone now, and I belong here. And I've had enough of the arts and entertainment business to last me a lifetime after all."

"Sounds perfect." Xandria said, "After all I will need your help around here, your wisdom and guidance as my oldest sister. And it seems we both belong *here* after all." Xandria thought of the sickness they each suffered—and maybe that was Oberia's way of calling its children home. Perhaps they each reach a point where the Outside Realm is too much for them to bear—even with all the Yasminea they can grow.

"Great," Maevis said, smiling more brightly than she had in months. "Just give me a day or two get things in order, and permanently retire from the Ballet Theater."

"Excellent!" Xandria said, "Take as much time as you need."

It was settled, then. Queen Xandria of Oberia finally found her destiny. She never felt at home in any other realm for that matter, outside of Oberia. She'd visited worlds full of murder and peril. And, lived in a world full of material possessions that dictate who a person is—educational degrees to justify a person's greatness in the world—or a size of one's home to justify who they are in society. Xandria's rightful home was a castle hidden behind a floral archway in the forest where she played when she was a young child. Sure, Oberia has its turmoil and troubles—albeit lessened now with the exile of her father's sisters—but they were ones she was suited to handle. And, she new Maevis was safer too; much safer, and healthier, than she had been in the outside world. They would never have to suffer the same fate as their parents. This was a consoling thought to Queen Xandria as she walked her sisters to the Gate.

"Fiona." She said, "Take good care of our father's company and his legacy. You've done him so proud, I'm sure."

"Of course I will." Fiona said, "I'll be back as soon as I can." Fiona smiled, but Xandria could sense her apprehension.

"Well if it ever gets to be too much," Xandria said. "You can come and help me oversee things here."

"Well, you seem so young to manage a whole kingdom by yourself," Fiona said. "But, with what you've handled this week, I'm sure it will be no problem." Fiona smiled and then let out a little laugh.

"Yeah, you'll be just fine." Xandria hugged her.

"I'll be back in a couple of days," Maevis said. "I promise." She embraced Xandria also.

"I know you'll be much happier here, Maeve." Xandria said.

"Oh, I'm sure I will." Maevis said, "I'm ready to leave the whole past behind me...Reese...my marriage to him...and even ballet." She sighed, as she let go of her sister. "I better go before I change my mind and leave Miguel wondering who on earth is supposed to perform in my place tonight." All three sisters laughed at that. Maevis went over to a large floral bush that bloomed right next to the archway. She plucked a large white blossom—looking like a calla lily, only smaller. And it smelled of a sweet, strong scent.

"Who is that for?" Cayden asked her.

"That nice young detective, Stan Browning." She said, "I um...I think he could use a little something to lift his spirits."

"But...that's Nalarah!" Cayden said, "Do you know what that does?!"

"Yes," Maevis said. "Of course I do. One smell of the blossom and he'll fall in love with the first person he sees." She giggled.

"But he's already crazy about you in the first place!" Cayden said.

"Oh dear, not me!" Maevis snickered. "Look, tomorrow I suspect he'll come to see you at school. He'll ask about me...I want you to give him this."

"But...but what if he falls in love with me?" Cayden said.

Maevis laughed, "Oh, don't worry. I've enough strength now to make sure that doesn't happen. I think there's a certain young teacher that could use a pick-me-up too."

"OOH!" Cayden said, "I see!" She grinned mischievously. "God, I love being a faerie!"

"Me too." Xandria said, embracing her youngest sister, "I want you to take care of yourself. And, behave in school."

"Oh, I will," Cayden said, "I think I should keep my pranks to a minimum. Giving people an elephant butt is a bit too much."

All four sisters laughed. Xandria realized Cayden was becoming more mature, ready to blossom from tomboy into a lovely young faerie with a good head on her shoulders. She was starting to learn the responsibilities that come with her powers after all. Likewise, Xandria was learning also as she faced her new responsibilities as Queen.

Then, after saying farewell, Xandria watched her sisters pass through the Gate into the Hollow. She sighed, feeling relieved that for the most part that this whole ordeal was over. The deceased human brothers-in-law, suspicious detectives, evil plots of ill-favored relatives…

However, Xandria knew that she had many more challenges ahead as a 19 year-old Faerie Queen. One chapter of her story was over, as another one begins.

One Last Dance

Fiona, Maevis, and Cayden stepped out from the Hollow and onto the path that lead to their house. By now the sun was right on the verve of setting over the westward hillside. "Wow, it has been a long day." Cayden said.

"It's been a long week," replied Fiona.

"I feel strong," Maevis said. Then she took in a deep, long breath. "Stronger than I've felt in a long time."

"That's excellent," Fiona said, "So, are you up for dancing tonight?"

"Oh, yes, my farewell performance." Maevis said, as they walked through the gate into the garden, where Yasminea blossoms were in full bloom around the wooden trellis. Butterflies fluttered around, drawn to the pink blossoms that sparkled with bits of gold. It was as if Maeve had planted their own little corner of Oberia in the Outer Realm.

Once inside, Maevis phoned the Theater, and asked to speak to Miguel directly. "Yes, it is me...Maevis." She said, as she sat behind her desk in the study. Outside the window, she looked as the sun set over the hills. Over the trees just beyond stands The Gate to her own Realm; where she would soon be dwelling with her sister. Home. She could hardly imagine what it would be like. As Maeve waited on the phone for the Artistic Director to answer, she remembered when she first fell in love with dancing. Her parents had taken her to see the ballet *The Nutcracker*, and she had begged them to let her dance. They took her to the ballet school the next day, and let her audition. She was 6 years old at the time. The stern, old dance matron looked down on her through wire framed bifocals, "Let me see what you can do." She said. Maevis danced with the natural grace and poise of a faerie. She got accepted into the dance academy that very day and was one of the best dancers in her class. She rose to the role of junior soloist by age 14; became a prima ballerina at age 18. Now, at age 32 she recalls dancers that had performed with her at that age. Most had already retired by now, suffering either from minor physical ailments or serious eating disorders. Some went on to direct, act, choreograph, and even teach whenever they were regarded as "past their prime." Since Maevis turned thirty, it was suggested that she had reached that point. However, she still looked youthful and still danced as well as she always had. Continual training to improve technique was not her only arsenal; of course a wish-spell or two kept her going and enabled her to dance better and better. Sometimes she actually felt a bit guilty about doing so, knowing that there were many other young dancers stuck in the corps de ballet, just waiting their turn to become principal dancer each season. But other times—like when Miguel wanted to promote his own protégé' who he was secretly dating—she would relish her continued time in the spotlight. She always knew however, that she would one day have to hang up her dancing shoes for good. That day had arrived. It was bittersweet—as was the conversation she had with Miguel that evening.

He sounded almost too shocked when she broke the news that tonight would be her final performance, and she was "Retiring at last," as she put it.

"But Maevis, this is so sudden!" he said. "And, we thought you'd never retire. We figured you would be a permanent fixture. Are you finally giving up the spotlight? I cannot believe it!"

"Well you should be happy, Miguel." She said, "You both should. You always wanted Bridget to dance this role, and you told me this was her dream after all."

"But...we'll miss you," he said.

"Ill miss you too....all of you. Don't worry...I'll be happy to attend all of Bridget's performances. I'm sure she'll do just fine. Give her my love."

"I sure will Maevis." He said. "And, best of luck to you."

"I'll be in shortly then." She confirmed.

"Okay, see you then."

She hung up the phone. "Last performance. Here at last," she sighed, running her hands through her auburn waves. She thought of Reese...Wondering what he would have thought if he was still there to witness his wife whose career he had supported, promoted, and financed finally give up the ghost. Then she thought about his betrayal; his death.

Yes, the show must go on, she thought to herself, *but most importantly life must go on.*

🌸 🌸 🌸

That night Maevis gave the final performance before hanging up her dance shoes forever. All three sisters sat in the front row; along with a tiny, frail woman with long wavy platinum hair, dressed in a long white cloak. She smiled up at Maevis, who she took her final bow and picked up some roses that were laid at her feet.

She received a standing ovation that night, and went home to pack a few things. She left instructions with Fiona about contacting a realtor to sell the house that she had once shared with Reese.

Yes, life does go on after tragedy. Maevis thought to herself, *and, life goes on after the curtain falls at the Theater...And, I'll walk through the gate into Oberia, knowing that's where I truly belong.* For her two sisters, life would go on as well....Two would return to the Outer Realm and the life they were used to, one would be Queen in the land she longed for.

Other books by K. Crumley:

Facets Volume 1
Anthology of horror and fantasy short stories.

Coming in June 2010:
Prophecies of Fire
Fantasy Novel
The first book in the Corithian Trilogy

Keep watching for updates on all of her future projects
www.dragondreamzpublications.info/aboutkcrumley

.

www.ingramcontent.com/pod-product-compliance
Lightning Source LLC
Chambersburg PA
CBHW070750120626
46557CB00002B/528